BOOK 5
in the
Second
Chances
SERIES

Believing Again

PEGGY BIRD

author of *Beginning Again, Loving Again, Together Again,* and *Trusting Again*

CRIMSON
ROMANCE

F+W Media, Inc.

This edition published by
Crimson Romance
an imprint of F+W Media, Inc.
10151 Carver Road, Suite 200
Blue Ash, Ohio 45242
www.crimsonromance.com

Chapter One

Portland Police Detective Danny Hartmann didn't try to hide her surprise at what she was seeing under the east end of the Hawthorne Bridge, one of the eight that span the Willamette River, linking the two sides of Portland, Oregon. It wasn't the dead body that startled her. If the dead man hadn't been there, she'd still be at home, asleep. What she didn't expect was what else was there—a small, well-hidden city of makeshift shelters and camping tents, inhabited by a population of men sleeping in the cold fall rain that was practically a daily event.

"I thought all the people from these homeless camps had been moved indoors." She looked around and tried to make a quick count. "There must be, maybe, a dozen and half people living here."

"Seventeen, to be precise," Doctor Jake Abrams responded. "And, yes, some people were moved indoors a couple weeks ago when your colleagues came through and shut down the camps after some ass-hat business owner complained. But the number of people who need a place to stay is always bigger than the number of spaces available."

Abrams had made the 911 call that brought the uniformed cops, crime scene techs, and two homicide detectives to the transient camp. "The camps reappear under another bridge as soon as the cops leave," he said. "The current iteration has been in existence for about ten days. I'm surprised you haven't had a complaint about it already."

"Sorry," Danny said. Other than as a reaction to the anger in the doctor's voice, she wasn't sure why she was apologizing. "I wasn't aware the Portland Police Bureau was responsible for creating this." She waved her arms to take in the whole transient city.

"Okay, Doc, let's go take a look." Danny's partner, Detective Sam Richardson, ambled over after talking to the two uniforms who'd responded to the emergency call.

Thank God, Danny thought. *Someone to change the subject and shut this jerk up.* She hoped her disgust wasn't too evident.

"He's…The body's over there," Abrams said, pointing to a shelter set apart from the rest of the camp. "I found him about six A.M., when I came to make rounds." Leading the two detectives toward what looked like an old plastic drop cloth over some sort of cardboard frame, he continued, "At first, when he didn't respond, I thought he was sleeping off a night of drinking. But then I saw this." They'd reached the structure surrounded by yellow crime scene tape, and he pointed to a series of holes low to the ground on one side that Danny immediately knew were bullet holes. "And when I looked inside, I saw he'd been hit several times in the head and neck and bled out."

"So you knew the man?" Sam asked.

"Yeah, his name is…was…Jim Branson. He's an Army vet. Served almost twelve years. Couple tours in Iraq, one in Afghanistan. Returned stateside about eight or nine months ago after he was wounded and discharged. I met him a couple months after that. Patched him up after a brawl. He had PTSD—post-traumatic stress disorder—and…"

"We know that one, Doc. We've seen enough colleagues with it," Sam said.

"Right. Sorry. Too used to having to explain it to civilians, I guess." He ran his fingers through his hair. "He drank too much, got into fights, and didn't take care of himself. I was checking on him because of an infected knife wound in his leg."

"You make rounds on these guys every day?" Danny asked.

"No, I can only get here about once a week." He sounded defensive, as if he knew he should be there more often. Danny felt a flicker of pleasure at making the good doctor uncomfortable.

He continued, "I don't usually treat the guys here, just check up on them if they haven't come back to the clinic for a follow-up. Jim is…was…an exception. He asked me to treat him here. So I did."

"And you called as soon as you found him," Sam said.

"Of course I did." Abrams made a face that clearly showed how annoyed he was to be asked the question.

Danny waited, repressing a smirk, anticipating the enjoyment she would get from watching her partner put the pain-in-the-ass doctor in his place. Sam was an expert at managing a witness with a chip on his shoulder.

"Didn't mean anything by it, Doc. Sometimes people try to revive the victim or look around for the perp and don't call right away. Just trying to get a clearer picture of how things happened."

Oh, hell. He's playing mild-mannered Sam. Where's the crusty one I know and love? Danny quickly checked the expressions on the faces of the two men to make sure she hadn't said anything out loud. She was relieved when the conversation went on without interruption.

"Sorry." Jake Abrams actually looked like he meant it. "Shouldn't have snapped at you like that. Guess I'm on edge. This is the third time this has happened."

"Third time *what* has happened?" Sam asked.

"Third time someone's shot into one of the camps. The other two times, no one reported getting hit."

"I don't remember hearing about drive-bys at a transient camp. Was it reported to us?" Danny asked.

The doctor snorted. "I doubt it. Why would anyone report it? You wouldn't do anything about it."

"Other than try and find out who was doing it, no, I don't imagine we would," she said, glaring at him. "I mean it's not like figuring out shit like this is part of our job or anything. So, of course…"

"Danny," Sam interrupted, "why don't you go talk to the guys who were within hearing range and see what you can find out? I'll stay here with the doc and sort out what he found when he got here."

Danny nodded and walked away, relieved to be out of the orbit of what was, she was sure, the snarkiest doctor—maybe the snarkiest person—in the city of Portland.

Ninety minutes later, she'd talked to most of the residents in the camp, two of whom she was surprised to find were women. No one had seen or heard anything other than a few strange noises that hadn't meant much to anyone.

A few of the inhabitants owned up to sleeping off too much booze. A couple said they'd heard noises that could have been backfires, gunshots, or their memories of combat. Most said there were always strange noises at night around the camp—cars and trucks overhead, people walking nearby, rats running around under the bridge. That made Danny even more grateful than usual that she had a warm, snug apartment to go home to. She hated rats.

She was about to rejoin her partner when Doctor Snark flagged her down.

"We got off on the wrong foot," he said. "I'm sorry. Can we start over?"

She waved off his apology. "Don't worry about it. I'm used to people not being real happy to have the police around. We deal with all sorts in this job."

He grinned and his smile lit up his face. A face that was really quite good-looking, now that she re-considered it. Wide-set blue eyes that looked as deep as the sea, dark hair that fell in waves around his ears and over his forehead, a bit shaggy, like he needed a haircut. Sculpted cheekbones, a strong jaw covered in designer stubble, and a full mouth that looked a hell of a lot better smiling than it had thinned into a line of disapproval. In fact, she couldn't take her eyes off his mouth, now that it was smiling at her. It was full-lipped and luscious looking.

His tall and nicely muscled body wasn't bad either.

"I imagine you do," he said. "I meet some jerks in my work, too. But most of the time I try not to be one. This morning I failed. I apologize." He ran his fingers through his hair. "My only excuse is that I get wrapped around the axle when it comes to these guys…"

"And women."

"You noticed. Yeah, and women. They mean a lot to me. And this has me worried. Like I said, it's not the first time we've had someone shoot into one of the camps. If it's the same person doing the shooting, they're escalating and that raises all sorts of red flags. It concerns me. Big time."

"Mind if I ask why this is so important to you?"

"A lot of the people in these camps are veterans, some from as far back as Vietnam, who've had a hard time coming home. I was in the National Guard. In Iraq." He paused for a moment, his eyes clouded, as if seeing something far away. "I know how it is. I volunteer at a clinic for vets. One of the things we do is try and get them to a place where they can really come home. Every part of them." He stopped again.

"Sounds like a tough job," Danny said to prompt him.

"Someone has to do it. The same government that sends these guys off to fight doesn't always do such a great job of making sure they get back to some sort of normal civilian life afterwards. They do okay for most vets but some guys slip through the cracks. Too many of them, in my opinion."

"You said the camps reappear because people have no place to go. Didn't I read about a VA program that provides rent vouchers for homeless vets?"

He nodded. "There is a program like that. Wouldn't be surprised if some of the guys here have those vouchers. What they don't have is a place to use them. Since the housing bubble burst, rentals are in short supply around Portland. The vouchers don't pay as much as the landlords can get on the open market so they limit the number of units available for the guys to use the vouchers."

"Thanks. That helps me understand what's going on a little better."

He looked down at her. "I guess I owe you one more apology."

Curious, she asked, "And what would this one be for?"

"I apologize for casting aspersions on the organization you work for. Apparently not all cops are disinterested in the problems these folks face."

"No apology needed. I'm sure if you rousted my friends out of their homes I wouldn't be too impressed with you, either."

The grin was back. "I don't think you were too impressed with me even though I wasn't anywhere near your friends' homes."

She shrugged her shoulders and smiled in return. "You could be right, Doctor Abrams."

"As long as we're starting over, it's Jake, Detective Hartmann. And you're…?"

"Danny. Happy to re-meet you, Jake." She put out her hand and he shook it, holding on to it longer than necessary.

"Danny? There must be a story behind that." The smile that went with the comment moved from merely attractive to downright sexy.

Dammit, he knew exactly what he was doing by continuing to hold on to her hand. "Not really. I like Danny better than my given name."

"Which is?"

"Danita, if you really have to know." She was not about to confess to trying to be one of the guys when she was a kid by turning the name she didn't much like into a boy's name. Needing to change the subject to something other than her, she grabbed onto the first topic that came to mind. "Speaking of names, I should have thought of this earlier but your last name is familiar. You have relatives who are doctors, too?" She managed to remove her hand from his as she asked her question.

"Generations of them. A tradition on both sides of the family. I followed one grandfather onto the staff at Kaiser. The other grandfather was on the faculty at the medical school. My mother's a pediatrician up at Doernbecher. My brother is a psychiatrist in Vancouver. My father's a surgeon at Emanuel."

"That's it. I think your father was the doc who put Sam back together a few years ago after he got shot up."

"He'll remember if he was. I swear my father can recall the name of everyone he's ever treated. And if Sam was his patient he'll be happy to hear he's doing great. Boosts his ego to hear how well his work turned out."

"Speaking of work, I better get back to mine. We'll be in touch. Promise me that if something, anything, happens that even vaguely seems like it's related to this, you'll call us." Reaching into her pants pocket she pulled out a business card and handed it to him. "My number's on here. If Sam forgets to give you his card, ask for it."

He scrutinized the card. "Hmm. No home address so I can come and roust you out."

"No, Jake. And don't bother with four-one-one. That won't find me either." She smiled before heading to the patrol car where the responding officers were congregated.

• • •

Damn. Why the hell had he been such an S.O.B. when he first met her? Now she wouldn't give him the time of day—unless it was the time she'd be at her desk, willing to listen to any evidence he might have. That wouldn't be the worst way to get back into her good graces. If only he could find something.

As he watched her walk away, he noticed that the rear view of the very attractive detective was almost as good as the view from the front. She was tall, maybe five-eight, five-nine. And she walked like she owned the place, a long stride with a controlled sway to her hips that wasn't sexual but was surely sensual. And those hips and fine ass were covered by chocolate brown pants that fit like a glove. The cream-colored shirt she wore looked good with her honey blonde hair and bourbon-colored eyes.

Where the hell were all the food images coming from? He wasn't hungry; he'd eaten breakfast that morning. Maybe not enough. Or maybe it was that he thought the lady looked good enough to eat. Although, she had a mouth on her that made him certain she'd be no lady when she was in charge of who was eating what.

He shook his head to stop this disastrous train of thought. The image of Danny Hartmann, on her knees in front of him, deciding who was eating whom, had to go before it took up residence in his head and distracted him for the rest of the day. He had surgeries waiting for him. Even food metaphors describing her hair and eyes were better than the very pleasurable image of her naked that was filling his thoughts and making his mouth dry.

"You okay, Doc?" Sam Richardson interrupted his fantasizing, looking concerned.

If Sam only knew how *not* okay Jake's thoughts about his partner were, he'd be more than concerned. "Yeah, I'm fine." Jake shook his head again, trying to clear it. "You finished talking to people?"

"Mostly. For now anyway. The patrol officers are about to leave. Danny and I will be around for another half hour or so. If you need to get to the clinic…"

"Nope, on my way to the hospital. I'm in surgery for most of the day but if you need me, here's my number." He pulled out his own card, tucking Danny's into his wallet as he did so. "Leave a message and I'll get back to you between cases."

"Sounds good. Is that Danny's card? I'll give you mine, too." Sam handed him a business card and looked as if he was about to walk away.

"Ah, Detective Richardson? One more thing, not related to what happened here. It's personal and I'll understand if you don't want to answer."

"Okay, what is it?" Richardson sounded very curious and a bit wary.

"It's about Detective Hartmann…Danny. Is she attached?"

"Attached? If you mean professionally, yeah, she is. To me. She's my partner. But if you mean personally, the only attachment I know of is to the classic VW convertible she restored and rebuilt from the engine out."

"Wow."

"Yup. That about covers it. She's a 'wow' kind of woman."

Sam had a look on his face that said he wanted to say—or ask—more, but he didn't, much to Jake's relief. Jake wasn't even really sure why he'd asked about her. It wasn't like there was a chance she'd be interested. Not after the way he'd behaved when they first met.

Fortunately, Sam merely shook his hand and walked away. Jake got out of there as fast as he could, kicking himself for behaving like an idiot, first with Danny, now with her partner. He needed to lose himself in his work.

Chapter Two

Danny didn't go all gooey-eyed over a man, no matter how good-looking or sexy he was. She thought women who did that were silly. She made fun of the females she and Sam interviewed who preened for him. Even teased him that no man well into his forties, happily married and the father of three, should put up with that kind of behavior.

Point of fact, she didn't spend a lot of time thinking about any of the men she came in contact with every day. First of all, she was too damn busy trying to do her job. Second, she was used to being around a whole hell of a lot of men, which had inured her to most of them.

Third, and probably most important, it was usually more trouble than it was worth to think about someone because he looked attractive or seemed interesting enough to get involved with. Her hours were long, her job was demanding. And no matter how charming or handsome they were, most of the men she'd met so far didn't understand how important her job was to her.

The only men who understood were other cops, and her one foray into that dating pool had been a disaster. With the schedules they had, it had been hard work making the time to see each other and when they broke it off after almost two years of trying, only making detective and moving to Central Precinct had made her comfortable about going back to being merely colleagues again.

No, it was easier to be businesslike with the men she met. She didn't really need a man in her life to make her happy anyway. What made her happy was her work.

Growing up she hadn't collected pictures of wedding dresses or named the children she planned to have with the as-yet unknown groom. She was more the pretend-to-be-a-snake-eating-Special-Forces-operative kinda kid. Her mother had despaired of her ever wearing a dress or learning to dance or, heaven help her, dating. Her mother had been homecoming queen in both high school and college—where she'd majored in English literature—and wanted her only daughter, her beloved Danita Rebecca Hartmann, to follow in her footsteps as a wife, a mother, and a college professor.

Instead she'd come within inches of getting Captain or Major or Colonel Danny Hartmann. The military had been where Danny was headed until a college professor piqued her interest in the justice system and police work. So, instead of watching her daughter go off to the Army, her mother saw her obtain a degree in criminal justice, move to Portland with a college friend, join the Portland Police Bureau, and make detective at a younger age than any woman in the history of the Bureau.

Danny sometimes felt her choices in life had put a strain on her relationship with her mother. It was part of the reason the move to Portland had been easy. Although her mother always said she was proud of her daughter and loved her, Danny was pretty sure she was just as happy living a state away in California where she didn't have to come face to face with her daughter's life on a regular basis. And Danny didn't have to explain it at the family gatherings and holiday dinners she'd avoided like the plague since leaving California. Her colleagues were her family. They understood.

That kind of determination and focus had gotten her as far as she'd come in her career and usually erased the memory of any guy she met ten minutes after she met him. However, this morning, in spite of everything she told herself about how important her work was and how unlikely it was that Jake Abrams would be interested in someone like her, he had managed to insinuate himself into Danny's thoughts. There was something about him that wouldn't leave her consciousness.

When she returned to Central Precinct, she had the urge to Google him—to find out about the veterans' clinic, she told herself. But as soon as she typed his name into the search box on the Google homepage she shut it down. This was stupid. She would ask him about his practice and what his deal was with the clinic the next time she saw him.

As to whether he was married, engaged, or otherwise paired up, that was irrelevant. Wasn't it?

Idiot, she chastised herself. *Let it go. You have work to do.*

• • •

Two days later, Danny was on her computer trying to catch up on her reports when she was interrupted by a deep male voice coming from over her shoulder.

"So, is it true what all those cops on TV shows complain about? You guys spend all your time doing paperwork?"

She turned to see a grinning Jake Abrams, his hands in the pockets of his jeans, staring down at her with a look she was sure could boil water. It certainly seemed to be moving her blood in that direction.

With the jeans he wore a cream-colored cable knit sweater over a red turtleneck. The other morning he'd been in dark trousers and a tweed jacket with a white shirt open at the neck and no tie. Very doctor-like. Dressed like this, he looked more relaxed, unruffled.

Hot.

It unnerved her to have him towering over her the way he was. He'd moved in so close she didn't see how she could stand up without bumping against him.

She tried to laugh off her uneasiness. "Yeah, our job consists of hours of paperwork, frequent stretches of painstaking legwork nailing down boring details, and the occasional moment of sheer terror. Although the sheer terror moments have decreased significantly since I made detective and stopped busting down drug house doors or pulling over strange cars weaving back and forth on the freeway. How about your job?"

Her attempt at humor managed to take the heat in his eyes down to a more manageable level, thank God.

"There are some similarities," he said. "The long hours. The paperwork. Boring administrative details, although not so much the legwork. And my sheer terror isn't worrying about what someone might do to me but what I might do to them when I have them on an operating table in front of me."

The heat reappeared in his eyes and an image flashed through her mind. She was spread out in front of him, not in surgery surrounded by a crew of operating techs dressed in scrubs but in a bed. Neither one of them was dressed. She could feel the mattress move as he lowered himself onto the sweet smelling sheets, saw his hand reach for her …

Shit. This had to stop. She felt flustered and said the first thing she could think of. "What's your specialty?" *Dammit. Next thing I'll ask is, "What's your sign?"* "I didn't think to ask the other day."

"Thoracic surgery. Didn't you Google me?" The smug smile was back. "I sure as hell Googled you."

Not sure if she was more embarrassed that he somehow knew what she'd been tempted to do or that he had done it himself, she said, "I doubt you found anything of interest."

"You play basketball for a city league team, you volunteer with the Sunshine Division at Christmas, you earned a commendation for outstanding service. No mention of a Facebook, LinkedIn, or blog presence, no pictures of a social life, a boyfriend, husband, or lover. Did I miss anything?"

She cleared her throat and squirmed in her chair. "So, a thoracic surgeon. A lot of call for that at the vets' clinic?"

Cocking his head, he smiled, as if to say, "I'll let you get away with not answering for now." Then he responded to her question. "I did graduate from medical school before I went on to cracking open chests. I can still treat ordinary ailments with the best Doc-in-a-Box clinic."

"But you must do a lot of trauma work in your regular practice. Is that how you ended up in the Guard?"

The flirty twinkle disappeared and a cool expression took over his eyes. He was deathly serious, his mouth a thin line. "That and a misguided sense of patriotism."

"What's misguided about serving in the military?"

"I learned pretty quickly that killing for your country isn't as patriotic as I had thought it was. However, I learned even more quickly that caring for the men around me was."

She was glad after the seriousness of his response that she hadn't made a smart remark about his dressing in the colors of the American flag. Instead she said, "I can tell your commitment to the troops stayed with you when you came home. And I bet that's why you're here. But I've been diverting you from telling us." She emphasized the *us*, trying to get the focus back on the professional, rather than the personal. "What can we do for you?"

"I stopped by to see if I could talk you into coming with me to one of the transient camps. I heard that a woman who was in the camp the night Jim Branson was killed slipped away before we got there. One of my patients thinks she might be able to help figure out what happened. I know her and I'm pretty sure she won't open up to me. I thought maybe she might talk to another woman."

Danny picked up a zippered leather case the size of a file folder, shoved a pen and notebook inside, and said, "Let me tell Sam where I'm going." In what she thought was a smooth move, she scooted her chair away from him so she could stand without being too close. Unfortunately he seemed to understand why she'd moved and grinned knowingly.

•••

Having offered to drive them to the camp, Jake led Danny two blocks away from Central Precinct, stopping beside a sleek black SUV.

"A BMW X5? Wow," Danny said, as she ran her hand along the side of the car. "These babies get great reviews. And it's an X5M, isn't it? I read they have killer acceleration."

"It does. But I won't show off what it can do while we're in the city, unless you swear you won't give me a ticket." He opened the passenger side door for her. "You a car freak? Sam told me you rebuilt a VW Beetle."

"Yeah, my father taught me to love German cars. And this one's a beauty."

"Yes. It. Is." He said each word with pride.

"Must be good to be you."

"Not always. But right this minute it is *very* good to be me." His smile was white-tooth dazzling, worthy of a model on the cover of a magazine or in an ad for some expensive men's cologne. "It's been a long time since the passenger in my vehicle has been prettier than the car."

"The woman in your life wouldn't be happy about that comment."

"My mother and Hailey wouldn't object to what I said, I'm sure. Wouldn't even disagree."

"Your mother? And who?"

"My niece. She's three. She and my mother are the two women in my life—well, two females. Hailey is hardly a woman. And I thought police officers were trained to be subtle about getting information out of people. You might as well have asked the question outright." Before she could respond, he said, "There's no wife, girlfriend, fiancée, or significant other."

Several emotions swirled around in her head. She was happy he wasn't attached, flattered at the compliment, and horribly embarrassed by the clumsiness of her inquiry. That made her both uncomfortable and smugly happy, a combination of reactions she didn't remember having together before.

For the ten minutes it took to get to the camp under the Burnside Bridge, they talked cars. Danny was only too happy to keep the conversation on a topic she loved, so she could forget her inept remark and keep herself from thinking too much about enjoying being with him.

Knowing how expensive his vehicle was, she was surprised that he drove right up to the camp. She wasn't sure she would be that trusting. But then, the men she'd talked to at the other camp had so much respect for Jake, it was probably the same here. And that respect would undoubtedly extend to keeping hands off his car.

"How many people are here, do you think?" Danny asked as they walked through the camp.

"About twenty."

"How many camps are there in town?"

"Now? Two of some size outdoors in the city proper, that I know of. You've seen them both. But that doesn't count the smaller places where a couple guys bed down or the vacant buildings where a half dozen or so people squat until they're rousted. Then there are individuals scattered around under overpasses and camped out in doorways. We try to get people into shelters when the weather turns but there aren't enough beds for those who want them and there are some people who don't want to come indoors."

"Do you keep track of all of them? The people who live here, I mean."

"We try to but it's impossible. They move around. Move to someplace else." He walked up to one huge box, some sort of large shipping crate from the look of it, the kind you only saw at the port full of other, smaller boxes. A door was cut into the front and heavy blankets insulated the top and sides against the weather. Through the open door, Danny saw a dim light and a blanket-covered floor. She thought she could see the outline of a person in the faint light.

Jake stopped a few feet back from the door and called, "Kaylea, it's Jake Abrams. Are you there?"

A small, compactly built woman holding a flashlight crawled out through the opening. She was dressed in jeans and a heavy sweatshirt. Her hair was pulled back in a ponytail. Given that she lived rough, she looked surprisingly neat and clean. It was hard to tell her age—her eyes looked like she'd seen a century of problems but her hands and neck looked young. Danny guessed she could be about her own age, around thirty. Her expression was wary, her mouth set in a hard line.

"Yeah, I'm here. Whaddya want?" she asked as she flicked off the light.

"I heard you were in the other camp with Jim Branson a few days ago. You know the police are trying to find out who shot him. This is Danny Hartmann." He put his hand at the small of Danny's back as he introduced her. "She's one of the detectives working on the case. I was coming here to check on a couple of your neighbors so I brought her with me. I thought maybe you'd talk to her since you knew him. Detective Hartmann, this is Kaylea Garwood."

Before Danny could say anything, the woman looked around nervously and said, "I don't know anything about what happened to him." She pulled the hood on her sweatshirt up over her head and started back into her shelter. "You're wasting your time."

Jake shot Danny a look that said "good luck" and took off for the center of the camp.

Danny knew she had to keep Kaylea from going back inside where she couldn't reach her. "I'm not here to ask about what happened at the other camp. I want to try and get a picture of what Jim was like. Sometimes that helps us figure everything out. Jake—Doctor Abrams—said he was your friend. I hoped you'd tell me about him. That you'd want to help us find who did this to him."

Kaylea hesitated, her back still to Danny. After a long moment, she said softly, "Yeah, he was my friend."

Looking around at the few curious men watching them, Danny said, "You know, I haven't had enough coffee this morning. There's a coffee cart in the next block. They have really good coffee. Want to walk there with me?"

The other woman turned, surprise written on her face. "You know about that place? The woman who owns it is nice. Never chases us away or anything. She even lets us have some of her day old stuff for practically nothing."

Danny grinned. "Of course I know about Jumping Joe Java. I know where every coffee cart is for twenty blocks in either direction from the river. Bouncing from one to another is how I keep going some days. Come on. My treat."

Chapter Three

The two women walked in silence for a block and a half. When they got to the coffee cart, the owner greeted both of them by name, fixed them cups of coffee larger than the size Danny paid for, and threw in two doughnuts the detective gave to her companion, claiming she was dieting. Kaylea wolfed the pastries down and inhaled the coffee while Danny sipped at hers and observed the other woman.

When Kaylea was finished eating, Danny said, "Tell me about your friend Jim."

Kaylea didn't say anything for a long moment. When she began to speak, it was in a quiet voice. She didn't look at Danny "We hung out together for maybe the past four months. He liked my shelter. Said it was cozier than his old tent so he stayed with me sometimes. He was kinda my protector because I'd told him what happened in Iraq. He wanted to make sure I was safe where I was living. Told everyone that if I got messed with, he'd mess with whoever did it." She wiped her sleeve across her face.

Danny waited while Kaylea took a couple deep breaths and composed herself.

"Most everybody was afraid of him. I wasn't. Maybe because I understand." After another long silence and another wipe of her sleeve across her face, she continued, "He had PTSD. From the wars. And then he'd been hurt—something was wrong with his hip—that's why he got out of the Army. But no matter what they did for him, he was still in pain. The two things together made him mean sometimes, especially when he drank. Which he did a lot, assuming he'd gotten his government check or had panhandled some. Got in a lot of fights. Last time he got sliced up with a knife." She stopped.

Danny prompted her. "Is that how he got to know Doctor Abrams? He went to the clinic to get patched up?"

"I'm not sure if it was that or from going there for the PTSD. But he wasn't going in any more. This last time, when he got cut up, he wouldn't go to the clinic. Wouldn't let me go there either. I had to find Doctor Abrams when he came around to check on guys."

"Do you know why he was avoiding the clinic?"

"All he'd say was there was something—no, some*one*—there he didn't trust."

"Was it Jake Abrams?"

"Hell, no. He's like some kind of god to all the guys around the camps."

"But not to you?"

Kaylea stared at Danny with a spark of life in her eyes for the first time in their conversation. She slowly smiled. "Wondered if I'd get that past you. No, not to me."

"Mind telling me why?" When Kaylea hesitated, Danny quickly added, "It's okay if you don't want to. It's not official. I'm curious."

"It's a long story. I'll put it this way. It's not because of anything he's done. He does good work. And he's always been straight with me and everyone else, for that matter. But I've lost the capacity for hero worship."

"Fair enough. I think I know what you mean. I sometimes feel the same way. Comes from seeing too many of the wrong kind of people in my job, I imagine."

The expression on Kaylea's face changed again, and softened into acceptance, if not trust. "I bet you do. See the wrong kind of people, I mean. Must not be very enjoyable." She finished her coffee and began to gather up their cups and napkins.

Danny got the message. She stood up and helped clear the trash away. "There are parts of my job that aren't fun, people who are a pain in the ass or worse. But meeting the other kind of people more than makes up for those times." She hoped her smile conveyed that she thought her companion was in the latter category.

"One last thing, Detective," Kaylea said as they walked back to the camp. "Jim talked in his sleep. Most of the time it was about Afghanistan and Iraq. Lately, though, he'd been talking about something else. I could never quite figure it out. It was all, 'What do you think you're doing?' 'That's crazy stuff.' 'I'll have to tell someone if you don't stop.'"

"You ask him about it?"

"Sure. But he said it was the usual. I tried to tell him it was different but he brushed me off."

They'd reached the camp and Danny noticed Jake watching them as they went to Kaylea's shelter.

She put out her hand to the woman. "I appreciate your talking to me, Kaylea. And I'm sorry about your friend."

"Thanks for the coffee," Kaylea said in a gruff voice and disappeared into her shelter.

Danny felt Jake standing behind her before she heard his voice. "You were gone quite a while."

"Just went for coffee. You finished making your rounds?" She could see he was holding his curiosity at bay, wanting to ask her about the conversation she'd had but aware of Kaylea's presence five feet away from them.

"Yup. We can go whenever you're ready."

As soon as they got to his vehicle, he said, "So, Kaylea. Did you talk about anything of interest?"

"You, for one thing. She said Jim thought the world of you, like all the other guys did. She's not quite as impressed. Fresh out of hero worship, was the way she described it. Seems like she's a bit skittish about you."

He sounded like he was swallowing a laugh. "I'm not surprised. She doesn't have a lot of trust in men in general. Not after what happened to her in Iraq."

"She alluded to something happening to her there but I didn't push about it and she didn't give me any details. I assume she was in the military."

"Yeah, Army mechanic. Good one, I understand. But she had a rough time on her last tour. She was raped. More than once. By the same officer."

"Jesus. Was he court-martialed?"

"No. He was her commanding officer and she didn't turn him in."

"What the hell kind of system lets that happen?"

"A fucked up one. Less than 10 percent of the rapes that occur in the military are prosecuted. And only two percent of these accused are convicted."

"That's appalling. Why…?"

Jake made an irritated gesture. "I'd rather hear what she did talk about, if that's okay, not what she didn't."

"Patience not your strong suit, Doctor Abrams?" Danny nudged him in the ribs with her elbow, trying to lighten the atmosphere that had gotten suddenly quite dark—as it always seemed to whenever he talked about anything connected with serving in the military.

She was rewarded with a half-smile, so she continued, "She said Jim had been avoiding the clinic lately and had told her to do the same. He said there was someone there he didn't trust."

"So that's it. I wondered why he only saw me in the camp. She say who the person was?"

"Other than it wasn't you, no. He didn't tell her. But he still wanted you to treat him so you're off the hook." She hesitated for a moment. "Were Jim and Kaylea…uh…Were they intimate?"

"I assume so. She asked for birth control about the time he started hanging out with her. I was surprised. When she first came to the clinic we did a full history, and asked about sexual activity so we could test for STDs if we needed to. She was adamant that she'd had no contact whatsoever with any man. I thought she might be a lesbian until the birth control request. Shortly after that, one of the nurses told me about what happened in Iraq. Somehow Jim found out and promised to keep her safe."

"She said she told him. And that's how she described him—as her protector. She obviously cared for him."

"Anything else interesting?"

"Jim had been having bad dreams and was talking in his sleep."

"That goes along with the PTSD."

"But he was talking about different stuff. Someone was doing something Jim didn't like and he was telling the person he'd have to report him if he didn't stop. If that was more than a random dream or a flashback to a war zone, it might be a motive for murder."

Chapter Four

Nothing was breaking for them. Not that Danny had ever thought this would be an easy case to clear. The members of the transient community wanted nothing to do with the police. They wouldn't even talk to a female cop who traveled with an escort they trusted—Danny almost always took Jake with her when she made a trip to the camp. She'd hoped there'd be someone with something worthwhile to tell her and a willingness to do so. It hadn't happened.

So far, she and Sam had unearthed only two pieces of potentially useful information. First, in one of the shootings Jake had mentioned that had occurred before the murder, a man *had* been slightly wounded. He'd gone to the ER and told them he'd been in a fight—consequently, the hospital report of a gunshot wound made no mention of a drive-by shooting into a transient camp. And no one at the camp had thought to tell Jake—or anyone else—about something that seemed to be only some random event.

And then there was tidbit number two. Around the time of the two shootings and the murder, a small, dark, maybe black sedan had been seen in all three locations. It had been variously described as a Honda, a Hyundai, and a Toyota Corolla—not exactly courtroom-worthy identification, but it was something.

Then, less than a week after Jim Branson's murder, another homeless veteran was shot and seriously wounded. He was on life support but not expected to live. Danny had been the first detective on scene. For seventy-two hours straight she worked the case, talking to people where it had happened, combing through the reports of the officers who'd first responded for anything she could follow up on, nagging the lab for results on the few things they'd picked up at the scene worth calling evidence. Every now and then she'd grab a quick bite to eat or catch the occasional nap, but she didn't go home—and had no plans to do so. She was determined to find something, anything, she could use as a solid lead.

Sam, who had been working as intensely on this as well as the other cases they'd caught, had at least gone home for a decent meal and a few hours of sleep each night. He'd urged her to do the same. But she stayed. Maybe it was the conversation she'd had with Kaylea; maybe it was that she hated to feel stymied by a bad guy, this bad guy in particular. Or maybe it was the pain on Jake Abrams's face every time she'd seen him.

But now, at the ragged end of three days, the fatigue was wearing on her. Tired, hungry, and caffeine deprived, she knew she needed to back off for a while. The coffee in front of her, which had started out as a cappuccino from her favorite barista, the one who gives good foam, was cold and about as tempting as the bagel beside it which was of hockey puck consistency. Promising to reward herself with fresh coffee and something decent to eat as soon as she was finished, she went through the crime scene photos once more.

Not that she hadn't done it about a hundred times already. And like all the other times, on this pass, nothing jumped out at her. She was beginning to think maybe Sam was right—she should go home, get some sleep, and come back with fresh eyes. Idly, she clicked through the images one last time before she took a break. First, the camp where Jim had been killed. Next, the site of the latest shooting. Then the images she and Sam had taken of the place where the man had been wounded.

Hell, this was a waste of time. She could have visualized the photos without the assistance of the computer. There was nothing new.

Wait. Something caught her attention as she clicked from one image to the next. *Go back, Hartmann, and see what that was.* She did, looking carefully at the photo. Then she went to the next image. Then another. Back to the first. Was it her weariness making her see things? No, it was there. Suddenly she was wide-awake and more alert than she had been in hours.

How could they have missed it?

"Sam? Want to come take a look at this?" she called to her partner.

He stood behind her and watched as she pointed out what she'd found. "I'll be damned. Nice, Danny. Let's call the doc and get him over here. See what he has to say."

In less than half an hour, Jake Abrams was standing where Sam had been, looking over Danny's shoulder at her computer screen. Sam was perched on the edge of her desk across from them, watching, gauging the doctor's reaction.

"Danny, why don't you show the doc what you found?" he said quietly.

"I've got two photos from each of the three crime scenes for you to see, Jake. What I want to know is whether you find something unusual in them."

First, she pulled up the images of the site of the drive-by, then the murder scene, then the most recent shooting. After the half-dozen images had been reviewed at least three times, Jake shook his head. "I see the camps the way I always see them. Grocery carts, tents, people. They all look alike." She could tell from the tone of his voice that he was frustrated. "I don't see anything different. Nothing I wouldn't expect."

Danny moved the cursor off to the side of the image, to a scattering of cardboard signs, the kind panhandlers use at freeway exits. "How about those signs? Anything there?"

Printed on the signs were pleas for money—some of them funny, like *I'll eat for food* or *Need money to buy a light saber because a Sith lord attacked my family*. Some were honest and asked for money for a beer or a hamburger; one even asked for donations for crack. Some were sad, if they were true—*Vietnam vet on the street after foreclosure* was the one that had gotten to Danny.

Jake looked them over and shook his head. Danny clicked on the computer and brought up the second image, pointing to a second set of signs. "Don't look at what's written on the signs. Ignore that."

It wasn't until the fourth image that Jake said, "In all those photos there's cardboard from East State Medical Supplies. Is that what you mean? I recognize the logo, and there," he pointed to one piece on the ground, "is the company's name on that chunk of cardboard."

"It's not only in those photos but in all the other ones, too. The only other recognizable names are grocery related. Those boxes are easy to get from any grocery store. But medical supplies? I wondered how the men got those particular boxes. Please, please tell me that company only does business with a few places in town," Danny said.

Jake laughed. "You're in luck, Detective. They've been trying to break into the west coast market by donating supplies to a couple free clinics in town. I think there are only two places where that cardboard could have come from: us and Outside In."

Sam put his hand up for a high-five with his partner. "Nice work, Hartmann. Now will you get the hell out of here and go get some sleep?"

Danny yawned. "Yeah, now that I found something worth following up on, I'll go. But I'll be back tomorrow and we'll go see those two clinics. I want to see how they handle their recycling and if anyone knows how that cardboard got to the camps. It may be it was simply given to them but I want to find out."

"I don't think we hand out cardboard," Jake said. "It's recycled into the bin out in the back every day where it's protected by a chain-link fence, razor wire, and a locked gate to keep people out of the yard. The recycle bin stays there except on collection day when it's on the street, right in front of the storefront window where we can see it."

"You're sure the gate in the back is always locked?"

"Yeah, we're paranoid about access. We have to be sure to keep all the doors and windows secure because we have drugs around that might be tempting."

"How about Outside In?" Danny asked. "Do you know…?"

Sam interrupted. "Don't worry about that. I'll go to Outside In and the doc's clinic. You go home."

Jake added, "Doctor's orders, Danny. You look asleep on your feet."

"Okay, okay. I'm outnumbered. See you tomorrow, Sam."

"Monday, Danny. See you Monday."

As Danny and Jake waited for the elevator, the full weight of her exhaustion hit her. She yawned and shuddered with the force of it.

"You sure you're in good enough shape to drive home?" Jake asked.

"I'm not driving. I took the MAX train this morning—yesterday—day before—whenever the hell I came in to work. I live over by the Lloyd Center."

"Then let me take you home. If you get on the light rail, you'll fall asleep and end up miles away from home in deepest, darkest east county. Assuming you don't get on the wrong train and wind up in deepest, darkest Washington County."

"You don't have to…"

"I want to. Please."

She closed her eyes and started to shake her head no, as she would have done if Sam made the offer. Then she changed her mind. This wasn't Sam hovering. It was Doctor Sexy playing nice. "Okay. Thank you."

When they got to his vehicle Jake opened the door and helped Danny in, pulling the seatbelt down for her and handing her the buckle. She fumbled with it, and the belt snapped back, snagging in the lapel of her jacket. He rescued her—or the seatbelt, she wasn't sure which—and smoothly pulled it across her body.

Even in her half-asleep state she could smell the clean, male scent of him, feel the warmth of his breath on her throat as he leaned over her to sort out the safety harness. As his hands deftly untangled the belt from her clothes, the backs of his fingers brushed against her breasts. She could feel a tingle and thought he felt something, too, because his sea-blue eyes went hurricane dark, and his breath hitched for a second…Actually, she didn't think she was breathing at all.

They were both frozen in place for a moment until he shook his head and clicked the tab in place, asking, "You okay?"

She nodded, her mouth so dry she was sure she couldn't have answered in words if her life depended on it.

Nothing more was said until they neared the Broadway Bridge. Waiting at a traffic light, Jake asked, "Where near the Lloyd Center do you live?"

"On Fourteenth, north of Broadway." She yawned again. His vehicle was so warm and cozy. She was so very, very tired.

He glanced over at her and patted her knee. "Stay with me. We'll be there soon."

Her body stayed with him but not the rest of her. She must have almost immediately fallen asleep because the next thing she knew he was shaking her gently, saying, "Danny? I'm on Fourteenth. Which is your house?"

She woke with a start. "Sorry. I must have dozed off." It took a few seconds before she could orient herself and answer him. "It's on the next block. Right-hand side of the street. The lower apartment in the duplex with the dark blue door is mine."

A minute later they pulled up in front of the house.

Without looking directly at him she said, "I appreciate the ride. Can I offer you a beer or a glass of wine? A cup of coffee? To say thanks?"

With his forefinger under her chin, he gently turned her face toward him. "I can't think of anything I'd like better than to spend time alone with you. But…you need sleep and I won't want to leave any time soon if I go in with you. So I think it would be best if I say no. But I'll take a rain check, if you're handing them out."

She was surprised at how disappointed she felt. "Okay, rain check it is. Thanks again for bringing me home." Impulsively, she leaned over and kissed him on the cheek.

Unhooking his seat belt, he slid closer to her. "I think we can do better than that, don't you?"

His arms tugged at her, bringing her closer. When she was only inches away from being pressed up against his chest, he took her chin again in one hand and carefully tipped her face up so it was close to his. All she could see, it seemed, was that full-lipped, sensuous, tempting mouth. She licked her lips in anticipation of what he was about to do with it.

But he didn't do what she expected. He talked. "You are one amazing woman. I've wanted to kiss you since the first time I saw you. Well, after I wanted to kick your butt for having such a smart mouth." He touched her lips with his finger. "Interesting. My first reactions to you all had to do with this." His forefinger outlined her mouth. "Now I'm finally going to find out what it tastes like."

The kiss started out slowly, his soft, sweet mouth on hers. That led to tasting the corners of her mouth with the tip of his tongue, then nibbling on the center of her Cupid's bow upper lip. After that, he got serious. With a growl deep in his throat, he urged her with the tip of his tongue to open to him, to let him in so he could taste all of her mouth. She acquiesced gladly, moaning a little as his velvety tongue swept through her mouth, expertly exploring every inch of it.

She melted against him, feeling her insides turn to hot, sweet liquid, wanting more than anything for him to take the next step, make the next move, whatever that was. The heat of his mouth, the passion of his kiss, seemed to have burned away her weariness. She'd never been kissed like this before, with such skill, such desire. She gave herself up to him, wanting nothing other than more of him because, oh, God, this man could kiss.

He clicked the release on her seatbelt then stroked his hand down her back, urging her to press the rest of her body against his. She went willingly, sliding across the gearshift console between them and snaking her arms up his and circling his shoulders. The kiss went on and on, taking her breath away, clouding her brain more than any fatigue ever had yet at the same time making her feel alert to every delicious sensation sweeping over her.

Suddenly she felt cool air on her throat. She opened her eyes as he gently kissed her temple, her cheek, the base of her ear as if reluctant to let her go even as he was pushing her away from him. "If you don't go in now, I can't promise I'll ever leave, and you need sleep."

She smiled and a small, soft laugh bubbled up. "Right. Sleep."

"And a rain check?" He ran his thumb over her lower lip.

"Yes, definitely a rain check."

He came around to the passenger side of the car and opened the door, leaning in for one more quick, soft kiss, filling Danny's senses again with the smell of his fresh, outdoorsy scent. She accepted the hand he offered and stepped out onto the sidewalk. Then she stopped. She didn't know what she was waiting for but her feet wouldn't move.

"Sweet dreams, baby," Jake said as he wrapped his arms around her and kissed her forehead. "I'll call you next week for that rain check."

Apparently that was what she'd wanted because suddenly she was able to walk up to her front door. When she got there, she turned to see him still standing by the passenger side of the car. He grinned. She returned the gesture.

After that kiss, sweet dreams are guaranteed, she thought as she unlocked her front door. But "baby"? She'd never let anyone call her that. Why hadn't she objected?

Maybe because when Jake Abrams called her "baby" it sounded seductively suggestive and she wanted to find out what it was he was promising.

•••

Jake arrived at his townhouse without knowing how he got there which was unusual for him. He was always aware of his surroundings, cautious about who was close to him and what they might be up to. Normally that made him a very safe driver. Not tonight.

He'd been surprised that first morning by how attractive he'd found Danny Hartmann. She wasn't the kind of woman he usually noticed, no tiny brunette with long hair and big eyes who looked to him for comfort and protection. Well, the big eyes she had covered in spades. You could get lost in those brown eyes. But her honey blonde hair was only a couple inches longer than his own shaggy locks. and Danny Hartmann looked to no one for protection, he was quite sure, with or without her Glock.

Although now that he thought about it, he'd never seen her with a weapon. He assumed she had one. As far as he knew, all Portland police officers did. Where did she carry it? He'd never seen her with a purse, only that leather case. Those form-fitting trousers she seemed to favor would show the outline if she wore it there. And he'd never seen her wear a shoulder holster. Although thinking about a shoulder holster nestled against those breasts he'd had pressed against him made him almost wish he were an inanimate leather strap.

She had a fine, fine body and looked like she worked out to keep it that way. Then he remembered what he'd discovered when he'd Googled her. She played basketball. He'd have to find out when she played so he could watch. *Please, God, let the team uniform be short shorts and a tight tank top, not that baggy shit everyone seems to wear on a basketball court these days. And while you're at it, God, turn up the heat in the gym so she sweats. I want to see the sheen of sweat on her neck and chest, like it would be if she were under me in bed, her body arched against mine…*

Holy hell, he didn't need to add yet another lascivious image of her to the ones he already carried around in his head. He forced himself to go back to wondering why she didn't carry a weapon all the time. It seemed a safer topic to think about. Plus, if he thought much more about her sweaty body he'd have to work on getting rid of one hell of a hard-on before he could walk in the house.

But it didn't help to change the PowerPoint he was playing in his head. Instead of thinking about what kind of weapon she carried, he started thinking about how she smelled. He didn't know how he got there from thinking about a Glock. He just did.

She smelled citrusy. Maybe lemon. Or lime. Clean and crisp. He wondered if it was some kind of shampoo. If he could smell her hair again, he'd know for sure. He wanted to feel it between his fingers, and brush those cute little bangs back from her forehead again, the way he had when he'd kissed her there. Or tangle his fingers in the back where her hair overlapped her collar. She didn't seem like one of those women who would hate having her hair mussed up. She wouldn't mind if a man—though it would take the right man, he was sure—messed with it.

It didn't look like she fussed with her hair or with makeup either. That first morning she'd had lipstick on. Today, nothing. But then, she'd been working for seventy-two hours straight. Not that she needed makeup. Even without sleep the woman was fucking beautiful. In addition to the body, the eyes, and a mouth he'd like to kiss forever, there was a glow to her, a confidence, which gave her a beauty mere looks couldn't begin to match. It was the way she held herself, the self-assured way she walked, talked, asserted herself. She knew who she was and what she was about and that was sexy as hell.

He'd wanted to ask her to dinner or drinks or something since that first morning but he'd hesitated to make a move, not sure if she'd be receptive. But that catch in her breath when he was buckling her seat belt was a tell. Even after working for three days straight, her body had responded when he'd accidently brushed the back of his hand across her breast. Her nipples had come to hard points he could see poking through her blouse. Not that he'd been immune. He hoped like hell she hadn't seen the erection that had appeared with the suddenness and intensity of the sixteen-year-old horny kid he used to be not the thirty-six year old he was now.

And then there was the kiss.

Oh, yeah. She was as interested as he was. He hadn't imagined the spark that first morning when she'd mouthed off to him under the bridge.

Then reality set in. Suppose she was like some of the others. Suppose she couldn't deal with what had happened to him. Was he willing to put himself out there again? It had been almost a year. Suppose she turned away, disgusted?

He sat in front of his townhouse for a long time thinking about the reactions of other women to him, the rejections and embarrassment. Danny wouldn't be like that, would she? Surely she was smarter, more sensitive. With a sigh, he got out of his vehicle and locked it up. Only way to find out was to try. But he sure as hell wasn't going to reveal it all the first time they were together. He wanted this to work. He'd take it slow.

But could he take it slow? Would she let him?

Next weekend. He'd ask her to have dinner with him and find out next weekend.

Chapter Five

Thank God she'd gotten some sleep. Monday morning proved to be everything Danny hated about that particular day—sorting out what happened over the two-day absence while also attempting to get a handle on the upcoming week's commitments and finding there weren't enough hours in the day to get it all done.

In addition to what would surely be a long court appearance mid-week, she was facing a shitload of witness interviews she'd promised Sam she would take care of for another case they were working. All of which meant that she had to ignore the niggling feeling she had that the killer of the homeless men was biding his time waiting to move in for another kill. Not that she could have done anything with the feeling anyway—they still had no idea what triggered him. Or who he was.

They hadn't gotten beyond what they already knew the victims had in common—gender, homelessness, military service, the Veterans' Medical Services Clinic, and probably the same weapon. With the cardboard ID'd as possibly coming from the clinic, it meant they should take a closer look there. But for what?

She had to get to the clinic, maybe the camps again, talk to more people. And she would, right after she found twelve more hours in every day and developed the ability to live without eating or sleeping so she could finish the "to do" list Sam had handed her and get the reports done for their other cases.

Then she got a phone call that rearranged her priorities.

"Hartmann," she said, probably more abruptly than usual.

"Wow, I thought a few hours of sleep would make you feel better. Apparently it didn't work," Jake Abrams said.

She laughed. "Yeah, it worked. Then I got here and saw what was facing me for the week. What can I do for you, Doctor Abrams?"

"What happened to 'Jake'?" he asked.

"Jake, please. It's been a long morning and it's only nine-thirty."

"Well, I'm afraid I may be about to complicate it further. Something's up with Kaylea. She went missing from the camp where you talked to her. I tracked her down to a different camp but she won't tell me what happened. Obviously it was serious enough to make her move again. She did say she was willing to talk to you."

"I'll go see her as soon as I…"

"This camp is not one I want you going to alone. If I could get her out of there I would. I sure as hell don't want you there."

"I appreciate the Neanderthal attitude. Sort of. Well, honestly, not really. It's my job and I'll be fine. Where's the camp?"

"I'll pick you up at any time you tell me and I'll take you there. I don't have surgery today and my morning opened up when I talked to Kaylea. My schedule is your schedule."

Danny sighed. She could tell from the tone in his voice she wasn't going to win. And her instincts told her this was important, she needed to talk to Kaylea. "All right. You drive. I'll bring the weapon and the handcuffs. Fair enough?"

"Your sarcasm is duly noted, Detective. What time?"

"Half hour, Doctor. Out front."

• • •

This camp was nowhere near a cramped, concrete bridge abutment. It was in Forest Park, the five thousand acre, city-owned, wilderness park which spread across the hills north and west of downtown Portland. After a hike from a parking lot at the edge of the forest, most of it through dense woods and thick underbrush that gave few visual clues as to where they were going—or how to get back—they came to the camp.

Not that she'd ever admit it to Jake but when she saw what greeted them as they walked into the encampment, Danny was glad she wasn't alone. The city's promotional materials said there were a number of species of predators in the park, including bobcats and coyotes. Had Danny been writing the copy, she would have added to that list some of the men she saw. One of the inhabitants of the camp actually leered at her and carefully ran his thumb over the blade of a rather wicked looking knife while he licked his lips and rocked his hips back and forth.

However, as soon as she squared her shoulders and looked the fucker straight in the eye, he dropped his eyes and took a step back. It probably helped that she'd been smart enough to leave her jacket in Jake's SUV and therefore her shoulder holster with the Glock in it was prominently displayed. Still, it was nice to have Jake walking behind her.

Besides, she would never have found the place without him.

The tents and shelters were in a heavily wooded area away from the developed running, biking, and hiking trails. Jake had said on the drive there that he'd found Kaylea when one of his patients had brought him to the camp but he'd been sworn to secrecy about it. The city didn't look kindly on people living in the park. In fact, the Parks Department had tried to shut down one camp about six months before but had only succeeded in moving a core group of people from one place to another, this time deeper into the woods.

The men who camped here had no intention of leaving and knew they had thousands of acres to play with. Everyone in Portland had heard the story of the man who'd lived in the woods with his daughter for years, walking across the St. John's Bridge to shop for groceries, unnoticed by anyone. That wasn't an isolated incident, either. There were stories of others successfully avoiding notice, living long-term in the park. The men in the camp followed in those footsteps.

In contrast to the places Danny had visited under the bridges, this one had a more permanent feel to it. People seemed to have staked out plots of ground for their living spaces. Everyone appeared to be sleeping under cover, unlike the other places where there were always a few who slept out in the open in a sleeping bag with, maybe, a grocery cart full of belongings beside them.

Here there were some rudimentary shelters with cabin-type bases constructed of rocks, logs, and branches, culled, Danny imagined, from the park's seemingly endless supply of downed Douglas fir trees. Atop the bases thus constructed were tents of all kinds, the bases giving enough height in some cases for the inhabitants to stand almost upright inside the shelter. Plastic sheeting or heavy tarps protected the campers from the wet; multiple blankets kept out the cold.

And there were amenities of sorts. Fire pits had been dug. There were battered pots and pans around a large cooking grate set atop a rock base. There was a creek nearby where several inhabitants were filling containers with water. Jake had already told Danny he'd gotten them to relocate their privies downstream from the camp and boil their water before they drank it. From the way he described it, there was more organization to this group, although it was not one he particularly trusted, especially with strangers. He said they'd been known to beat up hikers who stumbled into the camp to frighten them into keeping their location secret.

All the men—Danny didn't see any women in this group— seemed to be standing guard outside their shelters, watching silently as Jake and Danny walked through the camp. The expressions on the faces of those she passed were hard, unreadable, their eyes shuttered. These guys were tougher than the ones she'd met before. And, unlike in the other camps, there was no response to Jake, even from the few he spoke to by name.

When they reached the far end of the camp she spotted a familiar looking shelter. Stopping before they got to the entrance

Jake called, "Kaylea? It's Jake Abrams. I brought Danny, Detective Hartmann. Can she come in?"

From inside the shelter came, "Yes, but only her. No one else."

Grateful she'd worn a pair of jeans and heavy shoes to work that day in anticipation of getting the chance to canvass the downtown transient camps, Danny ducked into the shelter.

It was obvious Kaylea had tried to make the space comfortable. Danny saw the edge of a tarp sticking out from under the thick pile of blankets on the ground, which explained why the temperature underneath her wasn't too damp or chilly. What she assumed to be a makeshift sleeping bag was rolled up on one side of the space. A small box was upended in the center with a clay flowerpot and flashlight in the middle, the light beaming up to the ceiling of the shelter. There were several books scattered around the space— library books, from the labels on them.

"Hey, Kaylea. Jake says you wanted to talk to me. What's up?" Danny began.

It took Kaylea a few moments to begin, as though she was deciding whether or not to confide in Danny. Finally, however, she said, "You're looking for the person who killed Jim, aren't you?"

"You know we are. Can you help us with that? Someone else has been shot and we need to find this fucker before anyone else gets hurt."

Kaylea seemed to respond to the intensity in Danny's voice. "The person who killed Jim came back to the old camp. He threatened me. He thinks Jim told me something I shouldn't know."

"Shit. Tell me what happened," Danny said softly. She sat quietly as Kaylea told her the story. There wasn't much for Danny to work with in what she said but there was a lot of fear in Kaylea's voice as she spoke. Kaylea never saw a face, couldn't say who'd threatened her. But it had frightened her enough to make her run.

When she was finished, Danny said, "Are you sure you don't want to come into town and let us find you a room someplace?"

The panic in Kaylea's eyes gave her the answer before her words did. "God, no. It's too easy to find people in those places. It's better here. No one messes with these guys."

"But will they mess with you? That's what worries me."

"Bob, one of Jim's friends, is here. He said he'd look out for me." She brushed what looked like a tear from her eye. "And since they all saw that you and Doctor Abrams know I'm here, that'll help, too."

"I'd rather take you someplace safer…" Danny saw the set of Kaylea's mouth and eyes and changed course. "Okay, if this is where you want to be, I won't push you. But I'm gonna talk to Doctor Abrams and make sure one of us checks on you regularly. And we'll get you a prepaid cell phone. Today. I'll put our numbers in it so you can call for help if you need it. Make sure you keep it turned off to save the battery for when you need it." She got to her knees. "If you want out of here, call either Doctor Abrams or me. One of us, or my partner Sam Richardson, will come get you immediately if you want out. No questions asked. Understood?"

Kaylea raised eyes filled with tears to meet Danny's fierce gaze. "Why are you doing this, Detective? Don't you have more important people to help?"

"It's Danny, Kaylea. And right now, no one is more important than you are." Starting out the door, she wondered how she'd find Jake when she went back to the main part of the camp. She sure as hell didn't want to hang around here alone too long. But she needn't have worried. He was at the entrance in seconds after she crawled out.

"Anything I can do?" he asked.

"Yeah, we need to get a prepaid cell phone for her and put both our numbers in it. She wants to stay but she should have some way to let us know if she changes her mind. I told her one of us would swing by regularly and check on her, too."

"You're not coming here alone," Jake said. "I'll check on her. Or we can come together."

"Can we discuss this someplace else?" she asked.

They hiked out, found a convenience store where they could buy a cell phone, and took it back to Kaylea. On their second exit from the camp, Danny suggested lunch at her favorite food cart in Northwest Portland so she could tell Jake what she'd learned.

Over a bowl of what he agreed were the best soba noodles in the city, she recounted what Kaylea had told her.

Sometime during the last night she'd spent at the camp under the Burnside Bridge, Kaylea had awakened to a sound outside her shelter. She thought it was probably one of the men trying to get in to, as she described it, "mess with me," so she pulled out her weapon, a broken-off, jagged wine bottle, and waited. But the person stayed outside. The noises were odd. She couldn't place them. After about ten minutes they stopped. She was awake most of the night in case whoever it was came back.

It wasn't until the next morning that she found the blankets insulating one part of her shelter had been moved so someone could write all over the packing crate underneath. There were threats demanding she stop talking to the cops about what Jim told her or she'd be the next one sent to the hospital—or worse— even if she wasn't like the others. She thought that last part was referring to the fact she was a woman, not a man, but she wasn't sure.

What she was sure of was that she was scared. And no one in the camp, except for Jim's buddy, Bob, seemed willing to help. Everyone else swore they hadn't seen or heard anything and since she'd always had her shelter on the edge of the camp, it may have been true. Or they may have been protecting themselves. Or been too drunk to remember even if they had heard something.

With Bob's help, Kaylea gathered up her belongings and moved. He got her settled in Forest Park. He moved there, too, and promised to protect her.

When Danny was finished, Jake didn't say anything, staring silently at her long enough to make her uneasy. "What? Did I miss something?" Danny asked.

"Miss something? Holy hell, no. You got more out of her in fifteen minutes than I have in months of talking to her. You wouldn't want to volunteer at the clinic and work with the women vets, would you?"

"I appreciate your confidence, Doctor Abrams, but I think I should stick to what I do best—which is police work."

"There you go again."

"Go again doing what?"

His blue eyes positively twinkled. "It's still Jake. I don't intend to spend my rain check evening with you calling me Doctor Abrams. That's my father and he doesn't date anymore."

Chapter Six

Jake called Danny the next day and cashed in his rain check, asking her to have dinner with him the following Saturday night. When she asked how casual the place they were eating at was, he didn't mention the name of a restaurant, but merely said there was no dress code where they were going. She should be comfortable.

Taking him literally would have meant sweats and that seemed a bad choice for the evening. Instead, she selected her favorite—and most flattering—cream colored pants and a dark gold lightweight sweater that hugged her breasts and slender waist and had a scoop neck that showed a little cleavage but not too much. He was right on time to pick her up, kissed her cheek when she answered the door, then drove them to Northwest Portland where he pulled up in front of a row of townhouses.

"Is there a restaurant around here? I thought this was a residential block," Danny said.

"It is. None of the restaurants on Twenty-First and Twenty-Third seemed right. So we're eating here. Which is obviously where I live." He cut the ignition and grinned over at her. "But if you'll wait for me to come around and open your door, we can pretend we're at one of those places with a valet and do this by all the rules of etiquette."

"The rules of 1950," Danny muttered as he walked around the car and opened her door. When she got out she asked, "Do you order in at your restaurant or do you cook?"

"I'm crushed that you would think I'd invite you to my home for dinner and order takeout. Of course I cook." He didn't let go of her hand as they walked up the path to his house.

"This should be interesting. I've never had a man cook dinner for me before," Danny said. It wasn't her usual style but, for some reason, she didn't mind his taking complete control of the evening this way.

"I hope I live up to your expectations," he responded.

Not that it was what he'd meant, but the thought crossed her mind that he had already more than lived up to her expectations with one kiss.

At the top of a steep flight of steps, he opened the door to a stunning three-story townhouse. The open plan living room/dining room had warm cream-colored walls and rich hardwood floors—cherry, she thought—with large rya-type rugs in the center of each of the two rooms. Two couches covered in a dark gold fabric with a nubby weave formed a right angle to a gas fireplace in the living room. A dining room table of some slightly reddish wood similar to the floor, with clean modern lines, was set for two although it could easily seat eight. She could see bits of what looked like needlepoint covers in a colorful abstract design on the seats of the chairs tucked under the table.

Before she could finish unbuttoning her raincoat, Jake was behind her, his hands on her shoulders, ready to help her take it off. She swore she could feel his breath on the back of her neck as he slid the coat off her shoulders. As his hands made their way along the outside of her arms, slowly slipping the jacket off her, she shuddered from the simple yet somehow sensual act. He hung it on a peg close to the front door as she racked her suddenly overheated brain trying to find something to say that would cool off the atmosphere.

"You have a beautiful home, Jake," she said, looking around. *God, was that the best she could do?*

To her relief, the grin on his face indicated his pleasure at her reaction. "Thanks. It's taken me a while to get everything the way I wanted it but now I'm pretty happy with it."

"You did all this?" she asked, sweeping her hand to take in the two rooms. "Not some decorator?"

He picked up a remote and pointed it at the built-in cabinet at the rear of the dining room. Soft music began to play from hidden speakers as he motioned to her to follow him toward the back of the house. It was cello music, she thought, although she wasn't much of a classical music fan and wasn't sure. She did know it sounded as rich and lush as the décor of the house looked.

"Well, my mom and my sister-in-law did the needlepoint on the dining room chairs, but, yeah, I'm responsible for all the rest of it. I'd had enough of living like a frat boy with secondhand furniture that didn't match. So, when I got back from Iraq, I bought the place and gradually made it home."

She hadn't moved so he took her hand and pulled her toward the kitchen. "Can I get you something to drink? Wine? Beer? A cocktail? I'm making myself a martini." He opened a lower cabinet to reveal what appeared to be a well-stocked bar. "Want one?"

"Sounds good. I don't think I've had a martini since I was in college and thought it was the height of sophistication to drink from one of those glasses." She pointed at the two cocktail glasses he'd brought up from the shelf along with a shaker.

"Where'd you go to college?" he asked.

"San Francisco State. My roommate and I would save up our money so we could dress up, go to the Top of the Mark, and pretend to be women of the world. We were only nineteen and twenty, and I'm not sure how many people we fooled into thinking we were older and sophisticated but we had a good time."

"A cop with a history of law-breaking? Tsk tsk."

"Yeah, we were both criminal justice majors, too. Should have known better, right? But no one called us on it. Like a professor of mine used to say, there are only two kinds of people in the world—the caught and the uncaught."

"Lucky for your career you fell into the latter category." He went back to his mixing and she looked around the rest of the first floor.

There was a breakfast nook that overlooked a small garden on the side of the house and a sitting area with another fireplace at the back. Behind that, she could see a deck. The kitchen looked like a professional cook had outfitted it. An assortment of expensive looking pots and pans hung over the center island where the stove was located. The counters were granite and the appliances stainless steel. On the stove was a large, heavy-looking Dutch oven from which a delectable aroma emanated.

Leaning over, she inhaled, making her mouth water. "What's in here that smells so good?"

"Coq au vin. It needs another half-hour in the oven. I took it out before I drove over to pick you up so it didn't get overcooked."

He handed her a cocktail glass that held clear liquid and two olives on a toothpick. "Cheers," he said as he touched his glass to hers and, without breaking eye contact, took a sip.

For some reason, even before she had any of the drink, Danny felt like she was over the legal limit. Maybe it was talking about her college escapades. Or maybe it was the smell of the gin. Oh, hell, it wasn't either. It was this man. She didn't know how he did it, but between taking off her coat and the way he was looking at her now, she felt stripped naked. And she loved it.

So, feeling drunk and naked, she was standing in front of the sexiest man she'd met in a long, long time, trying to keep her mind from moving from "I like your house" to "I'd like to find your bed."

He kept staring at her, sipping at his drink, making her feel warm and wanting and …

She had to get her wits back, had to sit down before her legs collapsed or she launched herself into his arms so he could hold her up. Or hold her close.

"Shall we go sit someplace and enjoy our drinks?" she asked.

He put his glass down on the island counter and took hers from her hand. "One thing first." He drew her to him so there was nothing between them except a couple thin layers of clothes. "All week I've waited to have the chance to do this again. I don't think I can wait any longer," he said and he lowered his mouth to hers.

He didn't bother with starting slow this time; he blew right past finesse to hyper-drive. His mouth was insistent; his tongue demanded she join him. Not that she objected. It was almost a relief to know he'd been as affected by the chemistry between them as she was.

Their tongues tangled in a sensual dance, full of promise. As her arms circled his waist, he pressed his hands on her bottom and she tipped her hips forward, feeling his erection against her body, loving the feel of it, wanting to feel more of it. Their clothes felt like heavy insulation now, not just a couple layers of cotton. If only he'd finish the job he'd started by removing her coat.

She was already so wet. He was already so hard. Dear God, how were they going to get through dinner?

Dinner. Right. He'd made dinner for her. Maybe if she focused on that she could right this ship before it sank completely. Before *she* sank completely, swamped by waves of desire.

She made a weak attempt to step back from his arms but he wouldn't let her go, pressing kisses from her temple to her collarbone. His hands had now found her breasts, massaging, teasing her nipples, further fueling the craving that was racing through her veins like fire, flaming in her belly and turning her legs to jelly.

"We're never going to get to dinner this way, Jake," she whispered. "And it smells so good."

"Not as good as you smell, baby." His nose was in her hair, his hands back on her bottom, his erection now harder, thicker, more insistent as he pressed it against her.

One last try. "And our drinks. We haven't had our drinks."

"Why would I want alcohol when I can get drunk on the smell of your hair?"

She stepped back. "Well, what do you want to do?" *Please, please, please make it the same thing I want.*

"I want to take you upstairs, get you naked, and make love to you." He grinned at her. "Isn't that obvious? It's what I've wanted to do since the first time I tangled with you."

With a sigh of relief, she began to unbutton the blue shirt he was wearing. "Well, since you're the host and I'm your guest, okay. Works for me, as long as I get dinner at some point. I didn't have any lunch today."

Chapter Seven

Jake was still smiling when they got to his bedroom. He'd blurted out what he wanted before he could think about how she'd feel about his being so blunt. Why wasn't he surprised when she replied with equal honesty? He loved it. She didn't play games. She didn't act the reluctant virgin. She was responsive and sexy and surprising. Turned out, he like all three of those things in a woman, at least in this woman.

He'd made sure his bedroom was tidy and the sheets were clean before he went to pick her up because he'd planned all along to end up here. He hadn't thought they'd start out there but, what the hell. He pulled down the tan, brown, and black patterned comforter and the crisp cream-colored sheet, and rearranged the pillows so it looked inviting.

Apparently he took too long because when he was finished, she'd already kicked off her shoes and was beginning to undress.

"Uh-uh. That's my job," he said, stilling her hands. She dropped them and he slowly drew the hem of the top up over her breasts and shoulders. "Hands over your head, baby."

She grinned as she complied. "That's my line."

"Tonight it's mine," he said and the top was off and onto the floor. Unlike most women he'd ever known, she didn't draw her arms across her breasts, hiding them. She stood there, holding his stare, the remains of the grin playing across her luscious mouth.

He'd discovered another surprise. She wore a pale pink, lacy bra that barely contained her beautiful breasts. He'd had her pegged for the plain cotton kind. The contrast between the no-nonsense Danny and the pink lace was hot.

Her nipples were a darker pink and in tight buds, poking out through the lace of the bra. He didn't wait to get her bra off but took one breast in each hand, caressing, molding them, feeling the tips of her nipples harden as he cupped her breasts. They fit into the palms of his hands as if created for him.

Capturing her gaze with his, he murmured, "I want you to tell me if you like what I'm doing. Do you like being touched like this?"

"Oh, yes," she breathed out.

"And this?" he asked as he dipped his head and took one nipple into his mouth, sucking, teasing it through the lace. She didn't answer, only gasped with pleasure. Moving to the other breast, he heard her moan, sounding almost breathless as he did the same there.

Now he wanted to touch her skin. He reached around her to unfasten the bra, fumbling when he couldn't find the hooks.

She guided his hands to the valley between her breasts. "Front hook," was all she said.

When he'd rid her of the bra he started on the button and zipper to her trousers. Underneath she wore some sort of panties that barely covered the subject but which matched the bra. "You're one surprise after another, aren't you?" he murmured as he tugged at the panties to finish undressing her.

"Why?" She covered his hands with hers, stopping him from further explorations, her curiosity now apparently as aroused as her body.

"Lacy girly underwear. Who would have thought?"

She smiled—no, smirked. "You expected Kevlar?"

"You have a smart mouth, don't you? Give me a minute to get out of these clothes and we'll find something better for you to do with it than taunt me." He sat them both down on the edge of the bed and toed off his loafers. His blue shirt, khakis, boxer briefs, and socks followed.

When he was undressed, he pressed her down on the bed, positioning himself between her legs, still wearing a white T-shirt.

She pulled at the hem of it to get it up over his head, but he waved her off, taking her hands in his and pinning them beside her shoulders.

Ignoring the questioning look on her face he began to kiss her again until she was diverted from the subject of his T-shirt and making small, sexy sounds at the back of her throat, and pressing herself against him. Releasing her hands, he skimmed his over the curves and dips of her body. He wanted to acquaint himself with every inch of her, get to know every taste of her from her mouth and breasts to everything south of there. Then he wanted to get lost in her.

Moving one hand down her body he found the thatch of dark blonde curls at the top of her thighs. He could tell she was aroused even before he touched her. Moaning, almost keening with want, she bucked her hips at him but he only inserted a finger. She was tight, hot, and wet, slick with desire. "I love it that you're so ready, so wet for me," he whispered into the ear he was nibbling.

"I want you," she whispered back. "I want all of you."

"Oh, baby, not as much as I want you." A second finger joined the first, and with his thumb he found the nub hidden in the folds of her sex. Synchronizing his tongue in her mouth and his fingers in her sex, he moved in and out, slowly at first, then gradually, as she moved with him, increasing the speed until he felt her internal muscles clamp around his fingers as she called out his name and climaxed.

She nestled her head into his shoulder as he kissed her neck and the spot behind her ear that she seemed to like. When he thought she'd come down from her orgasm, he rolled off her body. She made a noise of disappointment that stopped when he picked up a condom from the bedside table and turned back to her again. Motioning to her to help, they ripped open the foil packet and he let her unroll it onto his erection, gritting his teeth to keep from exploding in her hand at her touch.

Her expression was sexy and smug as she tugged at him to return to her. When he was between her legs she wrapped them around his waist and rubbed her wet and wanting sex against his penis. "Please, Jake," she whispered. "Now."

She didn't have to ask again. He entered her slowly, wanting to feel every hot, slick, receptive inch of her, wanting to always remember what it felt like the first time he claimed her for his own. She arched her back to bring her body closer to him, rocked her hips against his, kissed her way down his neck to the base of his throat. Oh, God, did she feel good. Every place he touched her, every time she touched him.

Even through his T-shirt, he could feel her dig her nails into his lower back as they spiraled higher and higher but he didn't care. The only thing that mattered was the intense feeling of being inside her, of hearing her moan with pleasure at what they were doing. He was lost in a whirl of sensation as with slow, then faster thrusts he climbed to the edge of the precipice and, as she contracted around him, milking him rhythmically, he fell, taking her with him.

When they had come back to normal rates of breathing, he eased himself out of her and went to the bathroom to take care of the condom. He took a few extra seconds to compose himself before returning to the bedroom, knowing that, no matter how good the sex had been—and he sure as hell hoped she thought it had been as spectacular as he did—she would be asking him a question he didn't really want to answer but knew he had to.

From across the room he could see she was watching him with a curious expression. "Something wrong, baby?" he asked, crawling into bed next to her and pulling her so her back was against his chest and they were spooned together. He would rather not see her face when he answered the question she was about to ask.

She took his hand and nipped at his knuckles. "The T-shirt. How come you didn't want me to take it off?"

"Are you saying it have been better for you if I'd taken it off?"

"Hell, no." She squirmed out of his embrace and faced him. "If you can't read the signals well enough to know it was amazing for me, you're not very observant. It's not that. It feels like there's something you're not telling me and I don't like being the only one in the room not in on the secret."

He flopped onto his back and put one arm up over his eyes. She laughed.

That wasn't exactly the reaction he'd expected. "Something's funny?" he asked, not bothering to hide the hurt he felt.

"I'm sorry. I shouldn't laugh. But I think it's funny you still believe if you can't see me, then I can't see you."

"Is that what I'm doing? I didn't know." He lowered his arm but kept staring at the ceiling, not looking at her.

"Either that or you're trying to distract me from my question. If that's what you're doing, I think it's only fair to tell you I've been worked on, worked over, and talked at by some of the best trying to distract me. I don't distract."

"Goddamn cop training," he muttered. "All right, I'll answer the damn question." He turned toward her, took a deep breath, and said, "I kept the shirt on because a roadside IED tore the living daylights out of one side of me when I was in Iraq. The results aren't pretty."

"And that's it? That's all?"

"The few women I've been with over the past four years all seemed to agree that I didn't match their idea of what a lover should look like. Starting with the woman I came home to who, I thought, I was going to ask to marry me."

"Oh, hell. Are you serious?"

"As a heart attack. My almost-fiancée had my injuries to deal with plus my PTSD—nightmares, temper on a razor's edge, flashbacks. She couldn't handle it. Not that I blame her. I couldn't handle it, either. It was bad. We ended it about three months after I came home."

Danny nestled closer to him and put her arm across his chest, running her hand up and down as if examining him. "You said 'women' plural."

"Yeah, a couple other women. They didn't say it, of course. But after the first time we went to bed, they found reasons not to see me again." He kissed the top of her head. "So it had to be what my body looked like. Unless it's that I'm not good in bed…"

Danny snorted. "I think we can eliminate that reason from our consideration." She raised her head and stared at him. "So what was it about me that led you to believe I'd do the same thing? I'm not sure I like being included in that group."

"Nothing. I swear. You didn't do anything to make me think that. But I couldn't take a chance. I wanted—want—you so bad I couldn't risk it."

Her hand now at the hem of his T-shirt, she said, "Let me take this off."

"Danny, I…"

"No arguments, Jake. It's coming off."

He sat up, stripped the T-shirt off, and dropped it on the floor. He kept his eyes closed when it was gone, afraid to see the expression on her face. He didn't realize what she was doing until he felt her pushing gently on his shoulders. When he was flat on his back, she straddled him and, working from his waist up, she touched his chest, his left shoulder, and the inside of his left arm, running her fingers over each scar.

When he heard her whisper, "My god, look what they did to your beautiful body. You must have been in hell," he opened his eyes. What he saw wasn't disgust or pity. Her eyes were wide with, well, he wasn't sure. Maybe sympathy. Maybe affection. Certainly something he wasn't unhappy to see.

He watched as she kissed and caressed every wounded spot, beginning with the surgical scars and moving on to the half dozen other places where they'd dug shrapnel out of him. She didn't miss anything, dipping her tongue into the hollows where he'd lost muscle and parts of a couple ribs, softly stroking her fingers over the puckers in his skin where it had healed oddly.

If he'd had any tears left in him to cry over what happened, he would have shed them then as she made her pilgrimage from one spot to another, gently blessing each scar with her mouth.

But she wasn't finished. Before he knew what she was up to, she'd slid off him, and, continuing her ministrations to him, headed down his body, this time with kisses growing more sensual than healing with every inch. Reaching his navel, she swirled her tongue around it, before raising her head to look at him, as if asking his permission to continue.

"Oh, baby, yes, that feels so good." He could barely get the words out, she made him so breathless with her attention. The salacious smile she gave him made his cock twitch which she apparently noticed because she took it in her hand and began to fondle and rub it in a slow rhythm, a maddeningly slow rhythm. He could feel himself growing larger and harder with her touch and knew from the smug smile, which had overtaken the sexy look, that she could feel it, too.

Just when he was about to turn the tables and flip her on her back, she put him in her mouth. Her teeth sheathed, her tongue licking, her mouth sucking, he knew it would only take a few minutes to send him over the top if he didn't stop her soon.

"Danny, I don't want to come in your mouth. Please."

Giving one final suck on his cock, she slid back up his body. "Where do you want to come, Jake?"

"You know."

"Yeah, but I want to hear you say it."

"Inside you. I want to be inside you."

"I think we can arrange that," she whispered and reached over to the bedside table, where she picked up not one but three condoms. "Hmm, prepared for every contingency I see. I like that in a man."

He grabbed a condom from her, ripped open the packet, and rolled it on. Then he turned her onto her back, saying, "That's enough talking."

• • •

Still tangled in his arms and with her legs around him, she closed her eyes, avoiding looking at him, trying to settle her breathing—and her feelings—after the second round of sex. It had been amazing, like the first time, not just physically but emotionally. He'd taken her to the moon and back with his hands, his mouth, and his body and taken her breath away by making himself so vulnerable, exposing himself to her reaction as he had.

The story about his injuries could make a rock weep. And the wariness on his face when she'd taken off his T-shirt, afraid he'd be hurt again, had about broken her heart. How in hell could any woman have been so cold as to turn away from him after what he'd gone through?

He didn't want her pity; she knew that. But he'd been cautious about asking for her acceptance. When she'd forced his T-shirt off, she'd seen a strength she'd seldom known in anyone, man or woman. Hell, she wouldn't expose herself like that to many people, but his willingness to lower his defenses appealed in a way she hadn't known mattered to her.

She'd figured he would be fun to be with. Was even pretty sure, based on that first kiss, that he would be sexy as hell in bed. But there was more to her reaction than that and it alarmed her. She couldn't let this be anything more than a fun way to spend what little free time she had. She wasn't in the market for a serious relationship—she sucked at relationships—and she didn't know if he was interested either, not after what he'd described to her about his recent experiences. Besides, they both had ball-busting jobs that took up all their lives and then some. When would there ever be time for anything else? More accurately, was she willing to find the time? After working as hard as she had to get where she was, was she willing to slow down enough to let someone like Jake in?

On the other hand, she didn't think keeping it light and casual after tonight would be easy. They'd gone speeding from a kiss in the kitchen to this uncharted emotional territory where she didn't know anything about the terrain or the rules and wasn't even sure she wanted to know either.

She felt the bed shift with his weight as he moved. "Hey," he said softly. "You okay?"

Opening her eyes, she saw him propped on one elbow, peering down at her, a worried look on his face. It was now or never. She had to set the tone for the rest of the evening, maybe for the rest of whatever would be between them. "No, I'm not, Jake."

She swore his breathing stopped for a moment. "What's the matter? Was something…?"

Shaking her head she hastily said, "There was a promise made about dinner. I'm starved and all we've done since I got here is hang around your bedroom. I didn't even get the chance to finish my martini."

An amused look replaced the worried one. "Hang around my bedroom? That's what you call what we've been doing? Interesting choice of words."

"Well, I didn't want to get into too much detail since apparently I talk too much."

"Ah, this is payback. Gottcha." He untangled his legs from hers. Tracing a line from her forehead to her chin before briefly kissing her, he said, "If madam would like to join me in the kitchen, she can drink her martini while I finish up dinner, which will be served in about thirty minutes."

He sat up. She moved close to him, her fingers drawn to his back where she found even more scars, reluctant now to leave his bed even though she knew she had better do it while she could. "Okay, I'll get dressed…"

"Aren't you going to stay the night with me?" he asked.

"Oh, I hadn't thought…Are you asking me to stay?"

He glanced back over his shoulder and grinned. "Yeah, I am. I want to see if you're still so chatty in the morning. Call it a scientific experiment."

"How can I say no to science?"

"Good. Then don't get dressed."

"Dinner in the nude? You're joking."

"Yes, I'm joking. My mother would find out and there'd be hell to pay. We weren't even allowed to come to the dinner table bare chested, let alone bare naked." He disappeared into a large walk-in closet as he spoke.

Raising her voice so she was sure he could hear, she asked, "A—how would your mother find out? B—if I shouldn't get dressed but we're not eating in the nude…?"

He was wearing one terrycloth robe when he reappeared and holding another. "In answer to A, God knows how but she would find out. She has her ways. I've learned not to question them. As for B, here, wear this. I have multiples."

"For emergencies like this?" She took the robe, realizing when she wrapped it around herself that it was too big.

"No, as you can tell, it's my size, not yours. I have a weird aunt who gives my brother and me each a robe every year. Has ever since we were teenagers. We've tried to get her to stop but it hasn't worked. Apparently she believes that males are very hard on robes and need to have them replaced annually. We usually donate them to a shelter but I haven't cleaned out my closet in a while so I have a buildup in there." He gestured to the now closed closet.

Half an hour later, she'd finished her martini and he served dinner. She'd never eaten such an elegant meal dressed only in a robe. It was almost as good as the sex had been—the dinner, that is, not the robe. The coq au vin was delicious, as was the crusty French bread, the salad, and the perfect red wine. After they ate, Jake suggested they wait for dessert. Danny volunteered to help clean up the dishes. Then, when the kitchen was spotless, he admitted that she was the only dessert he wanted.

She was happy to volunteer for that, too.

Chapter Eight

Monday morning Danny was humming her favorite Blind Pilot song as she got off the elevator, and accidentally plowed right into her boss, Lt. Chris Angel.

He squinted his eyes at her and reared his head back. "Did I mistake the day? It's Monday, isn't it? How come you're so damn cheerful? Must have been some weekend."

"It was okay." Sure her expression would betray *how* okay it had been and invite curiosity, she moved the conversation to his five daughters, a subject she knew would divert him. "How about you? You have college kids home for the weekend?"

"No, we took the two high schoolers to Eugene to visit their sisters. I swear, with the amount of money we shovel into the University of Oregon for those three, you'd think the university would have champagne and caviar waiting for us when we visited." His smile was rueful as he shook his head. "But it *is* Monday, no matter how cheerful you are. And as soon as you get yourself organized I want you and Sam in my office to bring me up to speed on the transient camp murders."

"Murders? Plural?"

"Yeah, the guy on life-support died yesterday. Guess you were too busy having a good time to hear." He clearly had his own ideas about what she'd done over the weekend. And, judging from his comment, they were uncomfortably close to reality.

Sam was at his desk already. "L.T. wants to see us in a half hour, Sam. The second vet from the camp died."

"Yeah, I know." He looked her up and down. "You look remarkably happy this morning. Apparently he finally asked you out."

Sam, she knew, would not be as easily diverted as their boss had been but she had to try. "Who's he?"

"The doc. He finally made his move. It's about damn time. He's been sniffing around you for weeks."

"Sniffing around me? Jesus, Sam, you make me sound like a bitch in heat."

He had the grace to look abashed. "You know I didn't mean that. He's just awfully slow. I'd have asked you out weeks ago."

"Oh, for God's sake, don't even go there. That's too weird for words."

He was doing a poor job of looking offended. "What's wrong with me? There've been plenty of women who've thought I was a hot guy."

"Yeah, your wife—my friend—included. And none of them your partner."

"Since all my partners until you have been men, it's goddamn unlikely any of them thought I was a hot guy." However, he was not about to be deterred. "You haven't answered my original question although your need to move this conversation in another direction leads me to an affirmative answer. What did you do?" He was smirking as he asked the question.

Danny played it straight. "We had dinner."

The smirk changed to curiosity. "Oh? Where? Was it good? I'm looking for someplace to take Amanda for our anniversary."

She hesitated for a few moments. "He made coq au vin for me at his house."

"Christ, I don't need to ask what you did for dessert. I assume you were putty in his hands after that."

If she'd been prone to blushing, remembering what they'd done for dessert would have turned her flaming red. "When have you ever known me to be putty in anyone's hands, Sam?"

"You have a point." He waited for her to continue but when she didn't, he collected some notes from his desk. "If you're not going to give me any details, we might as well work. Let's go see what we can thrash out about this asshole who's shooting up the city's homeless. That way the doc can concentrate on the next meal he's cooking for you, not on worrying about his patients." And he headed for their boss's office.

Forty-five minutes later they'd hashed it all out and had decided a more extensive visit to the Veterans' Medical Services Clinic was in order. It wasn't merely the availability of cardboard sign material there that led them to that conclusion, although Jake's clinic *was* the most likely source. Sam had visited Outside In, the other place where East State Medical Supplies, Inc. had donated supplies, had seen their indoor recycling bins, asked who had access to the cardboard and concluded it was a less likely source because of their process of handling recycling. Not to mention that Outside In treated street teens, not homeless vets.

The determining factor, however, wasn't the cardboard. It was that all three shooting victims got care from Jake Abrams at VMSC. It was hard to know the significance of that fact. Had Jake somehow put his patients in danger? Or was someone trying to get at him through them? Did he know something he wasn't telling them or, more likely, did he have information he didn't know he possessed? If he did, how could they figure out what it was?

Sam and Danny headed for Old Town, the part of the city where many of the social services for the homeless were housed, and where VMSC was located. They planned to interview as many of the staff and volunteers as they could to see what additional information—if any—they could gather.

Sam had cruised by the clinic when he was checking out their recycling bins. Danny hadn't ever been there. She wasn't sure if she wanted Jake to be there or not. She was curious to see him working but she wasn't sure how they'd react to each other after a weekend that was pretty much spent in bed exploring each other's bodies. Merely thinking about their hot weekend together was enough to make her pulse pound.

But it could be awkward. She'd never been involved with someone she met through an investigation. Not that anyone suspected Jake Abrams of being the killer. They'd already established where he'd been at the time of all the shootings and it was nowhere near the homeless camps.

Still, Danny wondered if she should tell L.T. about her relationship with him. Riding the light rail to work that morning she'd debated whether she should ask Sam for advice. He and Amanda had first gotten together when Amanda was suspected of actually being a perp in one of his homicides. But she also knew that giving her partner any more information about her involvement with Jake would fuel his curiosity and make him ask questions she might not want to answer.

During the ride to the clinic in Old Town, she took a chance and broached the subject.

"Sam, do you think L.T. needs to know that Jake and I are… that we're…well, you know."

Sam grinned. "Actually I don't know exactly because you won't tell me. But I can guess. And my imagination's running wild."

Danny began to regret her decision to ask his advice.

Then he redeemed himself. "Seriously, I wouldn't worry about it. We've cleared Jake of any involvement in this other than as a source of information. I'd tell you to be careful with what you say to him about what we find but I know you'd do that with anyone you were with."

"Yeah, I would." She let out a breath she hadn't realized she was holding. "It must have been pretty complicated getting involved with Amanda when she was suspected of murder."

"Complicated hardly begins to describe it. But it worked out okay. I mean, how could she resist falling for the man who was not only the best looking guy she'd ever seen but who kept rescuing her from the guys who wanted to make her take the fall for them? I even took a bullet for her."

"That part I know. I was there, remember?" She snorted trying to suppress a laugh. "I wonder if Amanda would answer the question the same way?"

"She better. But let's get back to the original question—I only told L.T. about Amanda and me after she became a suspect. This thing with Jake and you isn't anything like it."

"Thanks. That makes me feel better."

"You're welcome." He was driving and glanced over at her.

She was sure he was about to say something else but a parking space opened up near the clinic and he turned his attention to pulling into it.

The clinic was in an old storefront and was obviously a bare-bones operation. The waiting area they walked into had an jumble of mismatched folding chairs and plastic patio chairs full of people waiting to be seen, institutional-green paint on the walls, chipped and cracked vinyl floor covering, and curtains on the side windows that hung limply with the exhaustion of too many trips through the washer and dryer. The large front windows were bare.

In what passed for an office, created by a couple folding banquet tables and a few file cabinets, sat a frazzled-looking, middle-aged woman behind the only new-looking piece of equipment in sight—a computer. In addition to working on that, she was juggling two phones and the demands of people who, Danny assumed, were staff members who wandered in and out of her workspace ad lib, dropping charts and notes into her inbox.

It didn't take Danny long to see that Jake was there. Dressed in a white lab coat over jeans and the cable knit sweater which seemed to be his uniform for working at VMSC, he was hunkered down to listen to an old man in a wheelchair tell what seemed to be a long and involved story. He didn't hurry the man along even though the front area was full of people waiting their turn to see someone.

The two detectives walked up to the receptionist's table and Sam showed his badge and introduced himself. "We'd like to talk to some of the staff," he explained, "one at a time. In a place where we have some privacy."

The receptionist snickered. "Yeah, right. So would I. But we're slammed right now. You'll have to come back another time."

From behind them, Jake said, "I don't think that's how it works with the police, Greta." Looking over her shoulder, Danny saw the huge grin on his face. "Nice to see you again." There was no mistaking that he meant Danny but he hurried to include her partner by asking, "How can we help you, Sam?"

"We're on a fishing expedition," Sam said. "We're about ninety percent sure the cardboard in the camps came from here. But no one we've talked to seems to know how it got there. They all say it just appears. We think someone here might be the conduit, wittingly or not. So, we'd like to talk to your staff and see if anyone here knows anything. It's the only lead we have so we're following up on it."

"Greta's right," Jake said. "The medical staff is slammed right now. But I can rustle up a couple volunteers for you to talk to and one or two of the support staff who can give you a few minutes. If you can make do with that for about twenty minutes, when the lunch line opens at the soup kitchen down the street, our patients will magically disappear and the medical staff will be available to talk with you. That work?"

"Works for me," Sam said. Jake directed him to the staff coffee room which no one was using because they were so busy and sent in the man who was in charge of handling the recycling and other waste.

When Jake returned to the waiting area, his eyes lit up with an amused expression as he said to Danny, "Now, what shall we do with you, Detective Hartmann? Got any good ideas?" In a lower voice, he added, "If you don't, I have a few."

The innuendo in his voice sent a shiver up her back and peaked her nipples. Thank God she had on a sweater and jacket that hid her body's instant reaction to him. "How about giving me a small private space and someone else to talk to. That should do it." She fought to keep from smiling. "At least for the time being."

"You know," he said, his voice even more quiet, "we never talked about what we were doing this weekend."

"I noticed. We were too busy doing things other than talking."

"Detective Hartmann, you are an astute observer."

"Comes with the territory, Doctor Abrams."

"So, this weekend? Saturday?"

"How about at my house this time. I can't cook as well as you can but you won't starve."

"It's not your food I'm hungry for, baby, believe me." By now he was whispering.

She looked around and was relieved no one seemed able to hear them, although one woman who averted her eyes when Danny caught her may have been watching. "Okay, then. Saturday at my house at six-thirty," she whispered back.

While Jake went off to find a space for Danny to use, she went over a clinic roster Greta provided for her. She was amazed by the number of people who worked there. The paid staff was small—an office manager, a doctor, a physician's assistant, and Greta, a jack-of-all-jobs with the title of "clerk." But over two dozen volunteers—doctors, nurses, medics, PAs, and others who did office work—made up for those small numbers. And that didn't count the board, composed of prominent doctors and local business people who set policy and raised money for the clinic. It was an impressive operation.

Their interviews with a couple volunteers brought out nothing new. When the waiting room cleared out as their clients went for lunch, the administrative and medical staff went, one by one, to talk to Danny or Sam. Only two bits of information seemed of interest. First, there was a division of opinion about the move to treat more patients with PTSD, which had occurred when Jake brought in two volunteer doctors with experience in that area. A few staff members wanted those patients left to the Veterans' Administration to treat—mainly, it seemed, because of the long-term nature of the treatment. Everyone assured the detectives the difference of opinion had been professional and in the past but still, everyone also mentioned it.

Sam reported the second bit of information. In his interview with a woman named Barbara Black, who identified herself as the CEO of the clinic (her actual title was office manager), she waxed eloquent on the skills of Adam Burns, the staff doctor who she referred to as "her doctor," and complained he'd been relegated to mere support staff—her words—when Jake and his two colleagues had joined the volunteer team. Black believed that PTSD patients were best left to the VA for treatment because VMSC had fewer resources, very little time to give, and more people who wanted care than they often had staff available to treat. She blamed Jake and his colleagues for what she described as "straining the clinic's resources" with their program.

In interviews with Danny, several people acknowledged that Jake and Black had gone head to head at first about the changes he wanted to make, especially in the treatment of patients with PTSD. The personality clash between them was downplayed as just the result of a long-time administrator who had ruled the roost until a Young Turk had come along. It had all been settled long ago and no one thought anything about it now.

Danny was curious about why the patients came to VMSC when there was a VA hospital on the hill near the Oregon Health and Sciences University. When she asked one of the volunteer physicians, he laughed, then described the experience several of his patients had when trying to qualify for care there. The men were eligible on paper, but somehow the system refused to accept them. After a dozen trips up Pill Hill to stand in long lines and argue with a bored clerk only to be refused treatment, they came to VSMC where no vet was turned away.

Others of their patients had received a less-than-honorable discharge—some, ironically, because of PTSD-related behavior—which made them ineligible for VA care. Some preferred being treated for minor illnesses and injuries close to where they lived or bedded down. And then there were some who'd had a bad experience being treated in a VA hospital and swore never to return.

It was easy to tell when the lunch kitchen closed at the mission down the street. The waiting area of the clinic was again inundated with people. Their access to clinic staff and volunteers now cut off, Danny mentioned to Sam that she was going to ask Jake to join them for a quick bite to eat, to run some information by him—although she recognized it was an excuse to be with him. So did Sam, if the raised eyebrow look when he agreed was any indication.

But Jake had to leave for patient appointments at the other clinic, the one where he actually got paid for what he did. Danny had to settle for lunch with her partner.

At least she knew she'd see Jake on Saturday. She began to plan the dinner she would cook as Sam negotiated through downtown traffic to his favorite hole-in-the-wall burger joint, swearing Danny to secrecy, as he always did, so his wife didn't find out how often he ate there.

Chapter Nine

Unfortunately, nothing about Danny's plans for dinner worked out the way she wanted. The grocery store didn't have the halibut she'd planned to serve so she had to rework the menu to center on the salmon steaks that were available. Then the pears she poached for dessert fell apart in the pan, probably because she'd misjudged how ripe the fruit was and cooked them too long. She made the from-scratch gingerbread she'd planned to serve with the pears and, after she got the pan out of the oven, ran to the grocery store yet again to get more pears only to find they were all too ripe so she had to substitute ice cream.

After that, the vacuum cleaner hose broke as she was getting the place presentable and the dust bunnies she was sucking up escaped back into the wilds under her couch. That she couldn't fix right away and it took longer to mop and dust the non-electric way.

It didn't take too long. Her apartment was much smaller than Jake's townhouse. It was all on one floor. The front door opened into a small living room with a smaller dining room behind it. Further back, a teeny kitchen was on the left and two bedrooms with a bath between them were on the right. The beauty of the place was that the original woodwork was still there, unpainted and in lovely condition. Danny had built-in bookshelves flanking an old coal fireplace—now converted to gas—in the living room and leaded glass over yet more shelves on both sides of the French doors between the living room and dining room. Several of the light fixtures were also original in the Arts- and-Crafts architectural style she loved.

She'd furnished it mostly from Ikea, which seemed odd to some of her purist friends who would have pushed for Mission-style furniture, but it worked for her—the clean lines of the pale furniture she selected lightened the overwhelmingly dark wood original to the house.

After changing the sheets on her platform bed in anticipation of Jake's spending the night, she softened the pristine, virginal white of the bed with a brightly colored blanket, brought in a dozen candles, and put out clean towels in her bathroom.

When everything was finally set, she picked up a book and headed for a long soak in the tub, only to get a phone call late in the afternoon that changed it all. Another vet had been shot, and Danny was the first cop called, since it was the weekend Sam had his two sons from his first marriage with him. On her way to the scene, she called Jake to warn him their evening might be a bit different from the one they'd planned. He told her he'd meet her at the camp.

•••

Because it was a cold and rainy day, most of the people in the camp under the Burnside Bridge were in their shelters to get out of the weather. Apparently, the gray clouds and dusky sky had made the shooter brave. He'd stopped in the middle of the camp, stuck a weapon out the car window—the same weapon used in the other murders, from the looks of the shell casings—and fired randomly. Panic had ensued both under and above the bridge, where hundreds of people were wandering through the Saturday Market.

Everyone scattered. Only a few people took the time to look at the car. Again, the description was of a dark sedan but this time there was agreement that it was black with an H symbol on the back. Danny walked away from one heated—and slightly drunken—argument over whether the H was upright and therefore a Honda or slanted and therefore a Hyundai. License plate ID was even less sure. One person said it was MLS, another MIS, a third MLC. No one remembered numbers.

That questionable identification, the shell casings, and muddy tire tracks were the only real information Danny got. There wasn't much to go on about the perp. He wore a dark Balaclava mask and a dark turtleneck, and was in a dark car on a gray day.

The victim had not been hit in the random firing. He had been hit running away from the shooter after the people in the camp began to scatter. Danny was sure the perp had fired to get people moving then singled out his target and shot him before speeding away.

Once again the dead man was a patient of Jake's at the clinic.

Obviously distressed that yet another of his patients had been shot, Jake stayed the whole time she was working on scene. He went from shelter to shelter, patching up men who'd been hurt in the melee, checking on those he knew had PTSD and might be having flashbacks from the gunfire, making sure there were no more wounded.

Finally, about nine P.M., after all the interviews were completed and everyone who needed to be had been treated, Jake walked with Danny to her car.

"I'm sorry our evening got screwed up like this," she said.

"No more than I am. But we still have a few hours of the evening left," he said.

"I'm afraid I'm too tired to cook dinner."

"I was thinking we'd go to my house, which is closer anyway, and I'd heat up the Hungarian mushroom soup I made this afternoon for my lunch. I have leftovers. Then maybe a soak in the spa tub."

"You have a hot tub in your yard?"

"A spa tub in my bathroom. Didn't you notice it last weekend?"

"No, I can't believe missed it. Maybe I don't deserve to be a detective after all."

"Well, we were pretty busy with other activities." For the first time since he'd arrived, his sexy grin made an appearance.

"So, you have homemade soup. You have a hot tub in your house. What other services do you offer, Doctor Abrams, for the wet, tired, and cold women you pick up under bridges?"

He circled her shoulders with his arm. "I may have a few ideas. I'll let you know when you get to my house. You remember how to get there?"

• • •

The soup was delicious. Danny sopped up every last drop with the French bread Jake served with it. When they were finished, he directed her to the master bathroom where, in a large room adjacent to where the shower and sinks were, there was a huge spa tub that looked big enough to have a party in.

She turned on the water to fill the tub then took off her boots and started to undress. No, she decided. Jake had made a point of saying that was his job. She'd wait for him. Although she couldn't figure out what was taking him so long. Was he doing the dishes? Should she have stayed and helped?

When he answered the question by arriving with an armload of candles, she said, "Candles? You're a secret romantic?"

Jake looked startled, maybe even hurt. "Is that bad? I thought … but if you don't want…"

She reached for two of the candles and put them on the ledge above the tub. "You're sweet, Jake. And it's not bad, it's wonderful. You surprise me, that's all."

"That's a change. So far, it's been the other way around." He started lighting the candles.

When he was finished, he opened a cabinet, brought out a stack of fluffy looking towels, and turned off the overhead lights. "I'm sorry we missed our dinner at your house," he said as he took her in his arms, "but I loved watching you work. You're very good at your job, aren't you?"

"It's more than just my job, Jake. It's who I am. Like being a doctor is who you are. And I can say the same thing about you—seeing you with those guys at the clinic really showed me the kind of man you are."

"And did you like what you saw?"

"Oh, yeah. I liked it very much." She stood on tiptoes and reached around his neck with one hand, pulling his mouth closer to hers. She set the pace for their kiss, urging his lips apart with her tongue, exploring his mouth when he complied. His hands slid down over her waist and hips to cup her bottom and pull her closer to him, to where she could feel the beginnings of his erection.

He broke away from her. "You know, if we keep this up, we'll be wasting a whole tub of hot water and we're Oregonians. We don't waste water and power."

She laughed with genuine humor. "You're right. I may be a native-born Californian but I've learned the Oregon way. We need to defer having sex until we've taken advantage of the hot water and the power we've used to heat it."

"Besides, getting you into the spa tub means I get to make you naked and wet." He took the bottom band of her turtleneck sweater and pulled it up. "I'm dying to see that lacy bra again."

She complied and he got his wish. But he didn't look long. The bra joined the sweater on a chair across from the tub along with her jeans and panties.

"My turn," she said and did the same with his sweatshirt and T-shirt. But she didn't stop. After unsnapping his jeans, she eased the zipper down and pushed his boxer briefs over his hips. When they were both completely undressed, she held onto him with one hand and stepped into the tub.

It was gloriously warm. She slid under the water and beckoned for him to join her. He shook his head. "I like seeing you like this. You look like some sea goddess. Or a mermaid."

Suddenly she felt shy, and had to fight the urge to cover her breasts and pubic hair with her hands, not a normal reaction for her. But his gaze was so intense, his words so passionate-sounding, she was embarrassed.

"Don't, baby, let me look."

God, how had he known what she'd been thinking? She put her hand out to him again and this time he took it. When he was in the tub he turned on the jets. For the first few minutes they sat wordlessly enjoying the sound, movement, and warmth of the water.

Then he pulled her over on his lap. She hadn't known how much she wanted to be there until she was. It felt like where she belonged, his arms around her, her head on his shoulder, and her face nuzzled into his neck.

The kiss that came next was as passionate as his words had been earlier. And with access to her bare breasts, he took advantage of it, massaging and caressing first one breast, then the other, pulling gently on her nipples so a zing of desire shot from her chest to her belly. She wriggled free of his embrace and moved so she was astride him, pressing her sex against his penis. Groaning, he rocked his hips into her.

"Oh, baby, you feel so good."

"Sure it's not the massaging jets?" she asked.

"What am I gonna do about that mouth?"

"I have an idea about that," she said as she began to slide down onto the floor of the spa tub.

"Oh, no," he objected. "This is about you tonight." Grinning at her, he lifted her up and set her back on his lap, reached over the side of the tub, and grabbed a condom. He handed it to her.

saying, "Here. You can open this and help me put it on. Think you can do that without any more wise-ass remarks?"

"I can try."

She could more than try. She got the condom on him and then raised herself on her knees on the bench where he was sitting. Slowly, holding his gaze with hers, she lowered herself onto him. She loved the way he shuddered when he had completely filled her. Loved the feeling of having him deep inside her. Loved the way he licked his lips before kissing her breast, like she was a tasty morsel he couldn't wait to get in his mouth.

It was intense. The massaging water, the feel of his mouth and tongue playing with her nipples, suckling her almost to orgasm, the slow and steady rocking of his hips moving with her as she rode him in an up and down motion.

She tried to slow it down, to keep it going, keep it from ending too soon. But her body wouldn't cooperate. In what seemed like no time at all, she could feel herself clench around him, felt him grow even harder as her climax washed over her and she called out his name before collapsing on him. He nipped at the heartbeat at the base of her throat and joined her, emptying himself into her.

It took a minute or two before either one was willing to move. She finally slid off his lap and sat next to him while he removed the condom and tossed it into a wastebasket she hadn't seen next to the tub.

He gathered her back into his arms and gently rocked her, as if to soothe her.

"Mmm. This feels so good. Thank you," she murmured.

"My pleasure. And I mean that quite literally." He kissed the side of her head. "Even if it was a week later than I'd planned."

"I wondered if you always kept all that close by," she said, indicating the condom, the wastebasket, and a second foil packet on the floor.

"No, it was for you. But we never made it out of the bedroom." He looked so proud of that fact she had to laugh.

"In how many other rooms do you keep a stack of condoms?"

"I think we've covered it. I'm willing to play if you want to have sex someplace else. But if it's on the dining room table or the kitchen counters, I'm warning you, it'll be strictly missionary. I don't want to be on the bottom on those hard surfaces."

"Sure, let the girl get crushed into the wood or stone. Nice going, Doc."

"Hey, I didn't say we *had* to do it there. Only telling you what the ground rules would be if we did."

The sound of her pager going off came from the next room. "Oh, shit. I have to take it." She scrambled out of the tub, wrapped herself in a bath sheet, and ran to his bedroom where she rummaged through her purse until she found her pager.

It was Sam trying to find her. She dug for her cell and called him.

"Hey, what's up, Sam?"

"I tried your house and your desk. No answer. You still at the crime scene?"

"Not exactly."

"Ah, you're with the doc."

"Sam, what do you want?"

"Well, as much as I hate to interfere with young love, I wanted to find out what happened at the transient camp today. Would this be a good time to brief me?" He had a smug tone to his voice she was only too familiar with.

She snorted. "No, Sam, it wouldn't. But you already knew that. Do you really need to know tonight or can I meet you first thing in the morning and do it then?"

"How about hitting the highlights then details in the morning?"

She complied then added, "So, I'll meet you at the Justice Center about nine and we can brainstorm, if you can get away."

"Nine works. Amanda can take the boys home. They have to go back to their mom early anyway for some family thing."

She was about to say good-bye when he added, "One more thing—well, two more things—then I'll hang up—are you in his bedroom on your phone and are you dressed?"

"Jesus Christ, that's way beyond your need-to-know."

"Ah, so it's 'yes' to the first and 'no' to the second question."

"This is why I don't tell you about my private life."

"What private life? You haven't had one in the three years I've been your partner. I have a whole lot to make up for here. And I'm an old married man living vicariously…"

In the background Danny heard his wife Amanda interrupt, "An old married man who's not going to get lucky anytime in the foreseeable future if he doesn't stop harassing his partner who happens to be my friend."

"Thank your wife for me. I'll see you in the morning." Not letting her partner get another sentence in, Danny ended the call.

When she went back to the spa tub room, Jake had gotten out and wrapped a towel around his hips, a look that suited him very well. The way he walked toward her reminded her of the way the cat she used to have stalked prey. It made her shudder and sent a swirl of desire around her belly.

"Sam curious about what you're up to?"

"Sam's incurably curious. But it's none of his damn business." She reached for him, running her fingers up through the hair on his chest to his jawline then the damp curls at the base of his neck.

"I don't care if he knows we're together. Do you?"

"That's not the point. If you give him an inch he takes the whole nine yards. He can't help it."

"He's very protective of you, isn't he?"

"We protect each other. That's what partners do—they have each other's backs."

Jake outlined her eyes, her nose, and her mouth with his index finger. "I'm glad it's Sam who has your back. It makes me feel better."

"About what?"

"About caring for someone who does such a dangerous job."

"I told you, once I got out of a patrol car, it got a hell of a lot safer. Many of the people I meet are dead. The ones who aren't are dazed or…"

"Or guilty of murdering one person already."

"Yes, that's true. But I have an entire police force at my back when I have to deal with them." She shook off his hand, annoyed he was pushing about the subject. "What happened to Jake the romantic? Did he disappear someplace? I'd kinda like to have him back."

"You want him, you got him. I'll move the candles to the bedroom. You are staying the night, aren't you?"

Chapter Ten

The next weekend was somewhat less complicated. Danny worked all morning on Saturday but wasn't called back on a new case. So she finally got to make dinner for Jake, although she had to recreate the menu yet again. She'd cooked the salmon steaks for a couple dinners for herself during the week and, sadly, a large chunk of the gingerbread had also found its way into her mouth.

Actually, the menu wasn't all that hard to figure out—the halibut was available this time when she went to the store and the pears worked out for poaching. Salad makings were always in season.

Jake had told her he'd bring the ingredients for martinis and arrived with the requisite gin, vermouth, olives, and two beautiful cocktail glasses, which he'd brought because he'd been appalled when she said she would serve the martinis in wine glasses. He insisted the glasses were to be kept at her house so they could be filled with the appropriate spirits anytime the urge hit her. Or them.

He mixed the martinis and, after he poured them into the glasses, wandered off to her living room to put on music. She was curious what he'd find that appealed to him but wasn't surprised when it turned out to be Pink Martini. Any music fan in Portland liked the local band with the world-beat sound.

She was plating the Marcona almonds, Manchego cheese, and crackers they would snack on while they had their cocktails when she heard him call, "Hey, how come you have this?"

"What *this*?" she asked.

He appeared at the kitchen door holding something she should have known he'd notice. "*This* this."

"It's a menorah," she said. "It's used to light the candles during Hanukkah."

He gave her a raised eyebrow and a half smile. "I'm aware of what it is, Danny. What I don't know is why you have it."

"My mother's Jewish. We always celebrated Hanukkah. She gave it to me when I went off to college so I could keep up the tradition."

"Your mother's Jewish? According to tradition, that means you're Jewish, too."

"I'm aware of what tradition says it means, Jake," she said, turning his words back on him. "But I'm not really Jewish. In spite of my mom's best efforts I was a Hebrew school dropout. We didn't belong to a synagogue because my father's Lutheran. Didn't belong to a church because my mother's Jewish. We did light Hanukkah candles. In the years when the two holidays overlapped, we'd do it in front of the Christmas tree. I guess because I grew up with both, I don't much believe in either. Maybe I'm missing the gene for religion."

"Being Jewish is more than a religion. It's a cultural identity."

"So I hear." She took a sip of her drink. "Shall we go sit down while you cross-examine me more about my spiritual and cultural background?"

He waved her into the living room and sat next to her on the couch. "Sorry. Didn't mean to come across like the Spanish Inquisition. The menorah was a surprise. I assumed you knew I was Jewish, my name gives it away. But I didn't know you were."

"Your name and the Star of David on the chain around your neck. And maybe if I'd told you my middle name it would have given you a hint. It's Rebecca."

"There are lots of non-Jewish Rebeccas. Now, if you'd said it was Rivka…"

"Actually, that's what my mother calls me." She sipped her martini. "So, are you culturally or religiously Jewish?"

"Certainly the former. Not so much the latter, although along with the rest of my family I belong to a synagogue."

"Beth Israel would be my guess."

"Your guess would be correct—from my great-great grandparents on. But I'm not a regular at services although every few years I give in to family pressure and show up for Yom Kippur."

"The best we did was the occasional Shabbat dinner and Passover Seder with my grandparents. And, like I said, celebrated Hanukkah. I bet you did it all, even were bar mitzvahed."

"Oh, yeah. Couldn't escape that." He laughed. "Or weekly Shabbat dinners and Passover with all the family—which is a big group, given that we've been in Portland since right after Lovejoy and Pettygrove flipped the coin to decide whether their city would be Boston or Portland."

He looked at her over the rim of his cocktail glass. "Why don't you come with me to my parents' house some Friday for Shabbat? I usually try to make it there unless I'm on call." He must have seen the panic in her eyes at the idea of meeting his huge extended family all at once because he quickly added, "It's not the whole tribe on Fridays, just my parents and sometimes my brother, his wife, and their kids."

"I couldn't do that," she said, shaking her head. She dropped her eyes to the glass she was holding so tightly she was afraid she might snap the stem.

"My family would love to meet you. They've been hearing about you for the last month and are intrigued. I've been told recently I don't talk much about my personal life and they're interested in the woman who's suddenly made an appearance in my conversation."

She wasn't sure she liked the smirk that accompanied the comment. "Like, what're you saying?"

"Oh, probably that I've been seeing this kick-ass woman who's beautiful, has a fabulous body, kisses like she knows what she's doing, makes love like…"

"Seriously, Jake? You're going with that explanation? Do you think that'll get you fed and fucked?"

The gin he'd sipped from his glass was suddenly sprayed all over both of them. As he mopped up the drink with the cocktail napkins she handed him, he said, "So, that's your plan for the evening? How very concise of you."

"It got the reaction I was looking for, at least." She finished the last of her martini, popped a couple almonds in her mouth and stood up. "Ready for the feeding part?"

"Baby, I've been ready for both parts for days. Lead the way."

The evening was a success and by the end of it, Jake had worn down her resistance. Danny agreed to go to Shabbat dinner with his family the first Friday they could work it out.

• • •

They woke the next morning to a gloriously sunny Sunday. After a sweet session of lovemaking, they cooked breakfast together. Danny was amused to discover she was finding any little excuse she could to touch him, bump into him, stand close to him. He couldn't keep away from her either, leaning down and kissing her cheek or the top of her head, trailing his fingertip across her cheek and down her jaw, his eyes blazing blue fire. She wondered if they were going to get through breakfast without ripping each other's clothes off.

Somehow they managed. After they finished the stack of pancakes and chicken sausages Danny had piled on each of their plates, Jake volunteered to do the dishes while Danny showered and dressed.

After their morning of bump and grind, she should have known that being naked in the shower was too big a draw for him. She wasn't really surprised when she heard the door to the bathroom open and felt a surge of cold air over the top of the shower stall.

"Whoever came in here, you should know I'm a cop and I'm trained in unarmed combat."

The shower door opened. "Oh, Detective, I'm petrified," he said.

She glanced down at his erection. "Well, part of you is."

Shaking his head, he turned her so her back was to his front, took the bath sponge from her hand, and picked up the bottle of body wash. "There's that smart mouth of yours again. Luckily I've discovered a way to quiet it." He nuzzled her neck and began a long, slow slide with the soapy sponge across her breasts and down her belly, lingering long enough at the apex of her thighs to make her writhe in his arms. "You like?" he asked as he moved down a centimeter at a time.

"Oh, yeah, I like." She wanted more than a sponge there, however. She wanted him. But he wasn't cooperating. So she eased her fingers under his and took control of the sponge, dropping it onto the floor of the shower. Then she moved his hand down between her legs. "But I like this more."

He rubbed his now-rock-hard penis against her bottom as he slowly, too slowly for her, inserted first one finger than a second one, into her hot, wet, and wanting core.

"Yes, please. More," she begged.

"I love it when you want me like this," he whispered into her ear.

"I want you more than you can possibly imagine. I've never wanted anyone the way I want you. I don't think I could ever get enough of you."

"Oh, God, baby, I hope not." His hips moved, rocking against her. His fingers found the sweet spot at the front of her vagina and the heel of his hand rhythmically rubbed her clitoris. He was driving her higher and higher, until finally she reached the top, almost falling with the power of the orgasm that raged over her like a wildfire. If he hadn't been holding her she was sure she would have been on the floor.

He let her regain her normal breathing rate before turning her around and staring deep into her eyes. "I mean it, Danny. I hope you never get enough of me. Because I'm never going to get enough of you. I'm falling in love with you."

A stunned silence followed his words. Finally she whispered in a hoarse voice, "Oh, Jake, don't do that. You have to know, I'm really not a relationship kind of woman and I don't want you to get hurt by something like that."

He looked crestfallen. "Are you telling me you don't have feelings for me?"

"Of course I do. You know I do. But love? That's way out of my league."

He drew her to him, held her for a long while. When she pulled back from the embrace she could see the hurt in his eyes and knew she'd put it there. So she did the only thing she could think of. Sinking to her knees in the shower she took his penis in her hand and began a slow and sensual massage, licking off the drops of salty semen that she'd aroused, getting lost in the smell of him, the taste and feel of him, pretending this was all it took to satisfy him, satisfy her.

She looked up and saw him watching her with his intense storm-dark eyes and knew that this was only a temporary reprieve from the conversation she was afraid to have with him.

• • •

The only other woman he'd said "I love you" to had immediately said the three words back to him. He'd been sure Danny would reciprocate too. Had he read the signals so wrong? No, he didn't believe he had. She showed him how she felt every time they were together, every time they kissed or held each other.

He didn't believe the "I'm-not-a-relationship-kind-of-woman" excuse. There was something else. There had to be something else. Did she love him but was afraid to say so? Did she really think they could skate along on the surface with a relationship that was only good sex and good company? He had to know but was afraid to ask. Because if he got an answer he didn't like he knew there was no fallback, no Plan B. He couldn't step back from "I love you" and pretend that hanging out, rolling around in bed, and cooking for each other was enough.

Danny had blasted into his life with almost as much power as the damned IED. In fact, with more power because instead of making him feel like hell, she'd made him feel more alive than he'd felt since before he went to Iraq, maybe since any time in his life. He didn't know whether that meant they could live happily-ever-after but he sure as hell wasn't willing to give up at the first obstacle and write off the possibility.

The only thing he could think to do was to go on with their day as if he'd said nothing. If she wanted to bring it up, which he doubted, they could talk about it. Until then, he'd keep it light and sexy. He'd give her what she seemed to want. For now. Until he figured out how to get past her barriers and into her heart.

Twenty minutes later, both of them were dried and dressed. They hadn't said much since the shower and he knew he had to be the one to start the conversation.

"It's such good weather, why don't we do something outside? There won't be many of these days before next spring. Unless you have work you need to get done."

She looked surprised—and relieved. "No, I cleared my desk for the weekend. And you're right about enjoying the weather. What do you have in mind?"

"You like to hike?"

"Yeah. I love Forest Park, actually, but won't hike there alone so it would be great if we went there. And maybe we could swing by and check on Kaylea. I know you've been good about checking on her but I've only talked to her on the phone a couple times and I'd like to see for myself she's still okay."

"A two-fer. You're on."

Chapter Eleven

They left Jake's vehicle at the Macleay trailhead parking lot and hiked for a couple hours, enjoying the feeling of being lost in nature in the middle of the city. Then, after a break at one of Northwest Portland's ubiquitous coffee houses, they headed for the transient camp.

Kaylea seemed nervous when they got there but said she was doing okay. Danny noticed a man watching them the whole time they were in the camp. She assumed he was Jim's friend, the one who was looking out for Kaylea, but she didn't have a chance to ask. She did notice that he immediately went to the woman's side as she and Jake walked away.

As they walked out from the camp, Jake said, "Anything strike you about that conversation?"

"Yeah, she was nervous. And that guy was watching us really closely."

He stopped in the middle of the trail. "I think I should go back but I don't want to leave you here alone."

"She won't talk to you, you know that. I should be the one who goes back."

"No way. Not alone. That place is dangerous."

She stared him down. "I'll go back to talk to her. You hang around the edges of the camp checking on the guys you know."

He glared back at her.

"Don't give me that look. This isn't up for discussion, Jake."

"Tough S.O.B., are you?"

"So I hear." She turned before he could say any more and headed back up to the transient camp.

But going back to see Kaylea didn't get Danny any more information. In fact, it seemed to make the other woman more nervous. Something *was* wrong but Danny was out of ways, for the moment, to find out what it was. She wrote it off to the looming presence of the good Doctor Abrams who, in spite of what he'd promised, seemed to be within a few feet of her wherever she went. It ticked her off, but she wasn't able to figure out what to do about that right now either.

She waited until they were well clear of the camp before she said anything to him.

"Jake, you can't stand between me and what it takes for me to get my job done. I know what I'm doing. Hell, I've been told I'm good at it. You're overreacting. Lighten up." She was walking behind him when she spoke and couldn't see his face.

He stopped suddenly and she ran into his back. "I'm not overreacting. I know these guys, their reputation." He faced her with a look of anguish and he took her hands, holding them so tightly it hurt. "You're not safe there."

"This isn't your call." She shook free of his grip and put her hands on his arms. "I don't take unnecessary risks. Let me be the judge of what I need to do. Please."

With a low moan, he pulled her to him and crushed her in an embrace that was more desperation than passion. "I don't know what I'd do if you got hurt because of something I should have prevented."

"It's not your job to prevent anything. You're my…lover.. boyfriend…whatever you are…not my professional partner. And I won't get hurt. Now, can we close this subject and get on with our Sunday? I need more coffee and I haven't even read the comics yet, much less any other section of the paper. And Sunday's the only day I have to actually read the paper."

"Okay. I'll let it go. For now." He turned abruptly and continued down the trail, but she knew the discussion wasn't over.

They hiked in silence until Jake's phone rang. From the puzzled expression on his face, the caller was unfamiliar.

He repeated "Hello?" several times before the caller seemed to answer. After he paused to listen, he said, "Who is this?"

Another pause.

"I'm not going to answer that until you tell me who you are. Do you need help?"

Pause. Again. This time longer.

"Please, tell me who you are and where you are. I'll come to you if you need help."

After several rounds of essentially the same conversation, he said, "Look, if you won't tell me who you are there isn't any point in continuing this conversation. If you really need help, the clinic is open…"

He jerked the phone away from his ear as a string of invectives came pouring out loud enough for Danny to hear, too. Shaking his head he ended the call.

Danny said, "Doesn't sound like your caller thinks much of you."

"No shit. They wanted to know where I was so they could come talk to me."

"I'm guessing you don't know if it was a man or a woman."

"Right. Sounded like there was an attempt to distort the voice, maybe something like the old tissue-over-the-mouthpiece trick."

"More likely something over the mouth of the caller. Especially if they're using a cell phone. Does the number come up on caller ID?"

He checked. "Private caller."

"If you'll let me take your cell phone in, we might be able to trace it."

"I'll think about it—too many people get hold of me this way for me to let it go for too long."

"But if we can trace the call…"

Danny never finished her sentence. From the direction of the forest camp came the sound of multiple gunshots.

With Danny in the lead they raced back to the camp, arriving to a scene of such chaos that it was hard to know what had happened. Danny called nine-one-one and ordered Jake to meet the responding officers at the trailhead. He reluctantly complied, after first making sure Kaylea's protector knew to watch out for Danny, too.

Danny was pissed that he'd lost precious seconds on something so irrelevant.

Kaylea was in her shelter, safe but trembling, ashen faced, and unwilling to talk. Danny moved on to check out the rest of the camp. No one interfered with her, seeming to accept her authority. She regretted that Jake wasn't there to see it.

What she found was a trail of destruction through the whole camp. Shelters knocked over, belongings strewn all over the forest floor.

And then there was the body at the edge of the camp. It looked like the man had tried to run into the woods to escape but had failed. Danny knew that the ambulance she'd asked for would be of no use.

She also knew he was one of the men Jake had identified as his patient and she had to wonder if Jake's phone call and this latest death weren't connected. Perhaps the killer had known Jake was nearby and wanted him to see this.

The shocked look on the faces of the two uniformed police officers and the EMTs who were led to the camp by Jake was exactly the same as the one she'd had on hers when she'd first seen the camp. The officers quickly roped off the crime scene with yellow tape. The EMTs, whose expertise wasn't needed for the dead man, made the rounds with Jake to see if anyone else had been hurt.

No one had been.

Danny convinced Jake to leave with the EMTs, arguing that she and the officers would be there for quite some time and it was absurd to think an unarmed doctor added anything to the protection she had from two armed cops. He eventually agreed but asked her to call him as soon as she got home.

The three cops spent the next several hours interviewing anyone who would talk to them, which, it turned out, was a hell of a lot larger number than Danny expected. But one man may have put his finger on why they were suddenly willing to cooperate. He said they'd all heard about the guy shooting homeless men and were even more eager than the cops were to get him caught. But they couldn't help much. All anyone knew was that the shooter hadn't come from the trail Danny and Jake had used but from deeper in the park.

As he had done in the Burnside Bridge drive-by, the perp first shot randomly into the camp, causing the panic Danny had found when she first got there. Then, when everyone was running for cover, he targeted the victim, killed him, and left.

The only person who wouldn't talk to Danny was Kaylea. She refused to come out of her shelter. She didn't respond when Danny asked to come in. She wouldn't talk when Danny went in anyway.

Her protector, whose full name Danny finally learned was Bob Aronson, said it was because she was terrified, which Danny had already figured out. But Aronson knew the reason. Somehow, some way, the killer had gotten the message to Kaylea once again, that if she talked to the police, told anyone what she knew, she would be the next victim.

And Kaylea had been on the edge of the camp, where this latest murder had taken place, about the time Aronson had heard the gunshots.

Jesus, Danny thought. *Does she know who this bastard is but she's too scared to tell me?* She had to get Kaylea to talk to her, had to find out what she knew.

As soon as she'd finished talking to Aronson, Danny went looking for Kaylea only to find she'd packed up her belongings in a couple garbage sacks, taken someone's grocery cart, and left. For where, no one knew.

• • •

The next few days were more discouraging than any Danny could remember in a long time. Visits to the camps under the bridges and in Forest Park were unsuccessful. In fact, at every visit to each place Danny noticed fewer and fewer residents. She and Jake had to hunt in Forest Park for the new camp—no one wanted to stay at the old location. Thanks to a patient, they finally found the new place but no one could—or would—give them any more information.

The only thing that seemed obvious was that, for whatever reason, the perp was after Jake's current and former patients— which shone the spotlight even more on VMSC as holding the key to figuring out who was doing this. Jake was on the verge of stepping back from the clinic as a way to protect his patients until Danny pointed out that the killer seemed to know who they were anyway and depriving the clinic of one of its physicians wouldn't help them find the perp any faster.

Sam spent several hours with Jake asking him questions about every single staff person and volunteer in the clinic trying to find something, anything, to hang a theory on about why this was happening and who was doing it. The only additional information he got was a list of names of former employees and volunteers to talk to, trying to widen the circle in the hopes of finding something new.

While Sam was doing that, Danny was canvassing under every bridge and in all the transient shelters, soup kitchens, and SRO facilities looking for Kaylea. But the woman had simply been absorbed into the shadow city of the homeless and transient.

Or, Danny was afraid, had fallen victim to the killer who could have hidden her body in any one of an endless number of places in Forest Park.

As a result of the intense investigation, Danny and Jake had little opportunity over the next couple weeks to see each other. They managed a quick breakfast or two and, once, dinner during the week but not much else. She saw him more in the course of her work than she did socially.

She missed him. It was hard for her to face how much she missed him and how, in such a short time, he'd become so important to her.

Although she'd told him she wasn't good at relationships, that was only partly true. It would have been closer to the truth to say she didn't have much experience with them. She'd never really had a serious one. Not once in all her adult years had she ever cared enough for anyone to think about long-term anything.

It wasn't that she was extraordinarily picky. It wasn't that she didn't enjoy being with a guy. She'd had a couple boyfriends who had hung around for a while, even a couple years. But there'd never been anyone she'd thought of in a serious, long-term way.

And it wasn't that she was soured on the idea of a long-term commitment because of some hang-up from her family. Her parents had a warm and loving marriage of almost thirty-five years; her brother and his wife had been married for half-dozen years and still acted like honeymooners, even with two toddlers around.

It was more that she wasn't sure she knew how to make it happen for herself. She loved her work and would never give it up. Ever. How did a career like hers play into a close and loving relationship? She'd seen her mother turn down an amazing offer from a prestigious university in another state so her father could stay in his position at the university where they were both professors because he was in line for the chairmanship of his department.

Seen them work around competing publication deadlines with her mother always graciously giving way to her father. She didn't think he asked her to do it. But she knew it always happened that way. Could she do the same thing her mother had done? Would every man expect that? Her brother seemed to. Her sister-in-law had back-burnered her career as an attorney to raise their children while her brother's academic star continued to rise.

It hadn't helped that some of the men Danny had dated had been turned off by the demands of her schedule, gotten pissed off when she had to cancel dinner or a movie night because she'd been called out. If they were like that over a date, how would it be when it happened on Christmas? Or a birthday?

And kids? She'd never even thought about that. How the hell did you paint kids into this picture?

No, having only casual connections with the guys she dated had been just fine. Until now. Until Jake Abrams came along and told her he was falling in love with her. What the hell was she supposed to do about that?

Chapter Twelve

The case got colder as the days went by. Many of the people who'd witnessed one or another of the shootings seemed to have melted away like the occasional snow that fell on the streets of Portland—here tonight and gone tomorrow afternoon. The only good thing about the case slowing down was that it meant Danny could finally make plans to have Shabbat dinner with Jake and his parents.

Leaving work early for a change, she went to New Seasons Market where, with advice from the staff, she selected a good bottle of kosher wine and a bouquet of flowers.

Jake picked her up at six and they arrived at the Abrams's home close to six-thirty. It was already dark and, of course, raining.

Strict Jewish tradition is to light the candles eighteen minutes before sunset on Friday evening—and there were multiple online resources to figure out exactly what that time was in every location in the world. During winter in the Northwest, it was a tough commandment to follow for working people who wanted to be observant. Sunset occurs quite early because of the region's more northerly location. Jake's parents, like many Jews, honored the custom of lighting the candles on Shabbat but were flexible about the timing.

A handsome woman in her fifties with dark, wavy hair shot through with silver met the couple at the door of the Abrams's West Hills home Not quite as tall as Danny, she was regal-looking, as though she thought she was six inches taller and towered over everyone in the room. She greeted her son with "Shabbat shalom" and a kiss. Then she hugged Danny and gave her a kiss on the cheek, too.

"Shabbat shalom, Danny. I'm Miriam Abrams. It's nice to finally meet you. Jacob has said such wonderful things about you."

Danny glanced at Jake who shrugged his shoulders and half-smiled. "Shabbat shalom, Mrs. Abrams. Thank you for inviting me tonight. It's been a long time since I've been to a Shabbat dinner."

"It's Miriam. And, yes, my son told us you observed Shabbat growing up. Please feel free to join us any Friday you'd like, with or without Jacob. You're always welcome in our home."

Wouldn't that be awkward, Danny thought, *dinner with his family without him.* As she handed over the bottle of wine and the flowers, she saw that Jake's half-smile was now a huge see-what-I-mean-about-my-mother grin.

They followed her from the entryway down a long hall with dozens of family photos, some of them quite old looking, on the walls. Danny stopped to look at one she was sure was Jake as a gawky adolescent but he refused to let her linger too long, herding her into the living room. It was a room furnished more for utility than style with a mix of what seemed to be antiques, maybe family pieces, and comfortable couches and chairs arranged to take advantage of the spectacular view of the city lights the large front window showcased. Danny immediately liked the person who had opted to let the city be the star of the room—the woman in front of her, she was sure.

"I'll go get Harold and have him bring drinks. What would you like, Danny? Wine? A cocktail? Jacob usually has a martini."

"A glass of red wine would be fine, thanks," Danny answered.

When Miriam Abrams had disappeared into the back of the house, Danny said, "What's all the smirking for, Doctor Abrams?"

"I love watching my mother doing her charming best to corral you into another evening here. You might as well get used to the idea that you'll be back for another Shabbat. She's a freight train when she's trying to get her way. Or maybe more like a force of nature. Don't try to fight her. You won't win. I've been unsuccessful all my life."

"At what, Jacob?" Miriam Abrams had returned, a man who was an older version of Jake in tow. He carried a silver tray with four drinks on it.

"Resisting you when you have your mind made up about something, Mom."

"Oh, that. Yes, it's easier to give in." She was laughing when she said it but Danny was quite sure she meant every word.

Danny smiled at Jake's dad. "Hi, Doctor Abrams. You probably don't remember me but we met when you were putting my partner Sam Richardson back together again a few years ago."

"Shot in the left shoulder. Three women—three very attractive women—sitting around in the waiting room to hear how he'd done in surgery. Oh, I remembered. But I didn't recall your name until Jake reminded me."

"Yeah, Sam's fan club was there. Me, Margo Keyes from the DA's office, and Amanda St. Claire. Amanda and Sam got married not too long after you patched him up."

"If he was well enough to get married and is still your partner, I must have done an okay job."

"You did a great job. His shoulder aches sometimes when he's tired or been sitting behind a desk too long but mostly you'd never know he'd been injured."

"Tell him I said hello, will you?"

"I will. And he sent his regards to you."

A half hour later, when the drinks were finished, Miriam Abrams rose. "How about we light the candles and say the blessing? Danny, will you join me?" she asked. Miriam led the other three to the dining room table where a loaf of challah, a bottle of wine, and two candles set in ornate candlesticks were waiting. The table was set with heavy-looking silver flatware, delicate china plates, and crystal wine and water glasses reminding Danny of dinners at her grandparents' home when she was a child.

The same smirk was on Jake's face as Danny gave into the inevitable and joined his mother in lighting the candles. Maybe she was spurred by the sight of the table, or maybe because it was imbedded from childhood but from someplace deep in her memory, she pulled out the words of the blessing and, to her own amazement, prayed in unison with Miriam as Jake's mother waved her hands over the candle flames, welcoming in the Sabbath.

> Baruhk atah Adonai, Eloheinu, melekh ha'olam
>
> Asher kidishanu b'mitz'votav v'tzivanu
>
> L'had'lik near shel Shabbat. Amein

When Danny looked up, she saw the smirk was gone from Jake's face. The expression that replaced it was one of—well, the word that came to mind was "love."

Directed to a place at the table next to Jake, she sat down and he circled her shoulders with his arm. She leaned into the embrace and he gently kissed her forehead. He didn't say anything. He didn't have to. She was sure the candlelight was reflecting off the tears welled up in her eyes as brightly as it was reflecting off the water in his.

The ritual continued through the wine, hand washing, and breaking of bread. When it was completed, dinner was served—Caesar salad, roast chicken with a dried cherry sauce, roasted potatoes, and green beans with mushrooms. It was delicious.

Almost as good as the conversation around the table. At first Danny didn't participate much as she listened to the three Abramses discuss local politics. Eventually, however, she had to weigh in when they started talking about some of the challenges facing the city, including the problems the Police Bureau had with funding programs to deal with the mentally ill, some of whom often had more contact with law enforcement than with medical care. It was a situation everyone in the room agreed was untenable.

She'd forgotten how enjoyable a family dinner could be. The evening reminded her of the dinner table conversations her family had when two college professors and two teenagers, Danny and her brother, dissected current events, pop culture, serious literature, and anything else they wanted to talk about. Just like the Abrams family obviously did.

It was close to nine by the time they cleared the table. Danny insisted she help load the dishwasher after they had chased Jake and his father out with cups of coffee. She and Jake's mother worked in companionable silence for a bit, then Miriam said, "I don't want to embarrass you but I have to tell you how happy my son has been since he's been seeing you, Danny."

"Oh. Really?" Danny was uncomfortably aware of the inadequacy of her reply.

Miriam continued to load dinner plates into the dishwasher. "Jacob went to Iraq one man and came home another. Since he's been seeing you, he's more like the one who went there. And that's a good thing."

"I don't really think I can take credit for…"

"I'm not trying to put pressure on you. I know how relationships go." She sighed as she turned to face Danny. "But I appreciate having my son back, even if it's only for a short time. I've missed him."

Before Danny could think of a response, much less give it, Jake came into the kitchen with two empty coffee cups.

"I'm here to free the enslaved. Time to get you out of here, Danny, before she has you mopping floors."

"So, now you think you're Moses do you, Jacob, freeing your people?"

"No, Mom, just a man trying to save his date from having to do any more manual labor." He leaned down and kissed the top of his mother's head.

She beamed up at him. "All right, then, if you must. Take this beautiful woman home. But make sure you bring her back. Soon."

•••

The drive to Jake's house, where they were spending the weekend, was quiet, both of them lost in thought. At least Danny assumed Jake was as lost as she was. The evening had brought back things she'd deliberately pushed out of her consciousness. Like how comfortable it was to be included in a family. Like how moving it was to be part of a tradition as old as time. She loved her own home and she was always happy when she had dinner at Sam and Amanda's house. But tonight had been something special.

Maybe it was because she felt more like Danita Rebecca tonight, the girl who came from a close and happy family, the one the woman *Danny* had distanced herself from for some time. Shabbat with the Abrams felt good. She liked Jake's parents, liked the easy relationship they had with each other and with their son, the love she could feel around that table. The only thing was, it was forcing her to face the reality that she was beginning to feel the same thing for Jake he said he felt for her, even though she swore she never would, never could.

How could she be in love with Jake and be who she wanted to be? She was *Detective* Danny Hartmann, strong and independent, the kick-ass woman even Jake acknowledged she was. Being partners with Sam was one thing. He wanted her to have his back in a tough situation. Being partners with someone who might want something else, like putting him first or being there every night for dinner, was different. Different and impossible. Wasn't it?

As soon as they got into the house, Jake took her in his arms. "Thank you for going with me tonight. It was…magic." He gave her a soft kiss.

"I should be the one saying 'thank you.' It was the best evening I've had in I don't know how long."

"Really?" He looked down at her with a frown. "I thought we've had some pretty spectacular evenings in the past couple months."

"You know what I mean." She nestled her head into his shoulder. "I haven't felt part of a family like that in years. I'd forgotten how good it feels. Your parents are great."

"Annoying and intrusive at times, but, on the whole, more than passable, I agree." He lifted her chin up so she was looking directly into his eyes. "They like you. Which is no surprise. They knew how much I cared for you and they were prepared to like you because of that. But you…you blew them away. Like you blew me away from the very first time I met you. Still blow me away." He paused for a few heartbeats. "Danny, I'm not beginning to fall for you—I love you. Flat out love you."

She started to respond but he put his fingers across her lips.

"Hush. Let me finish. It comes with no strings. No requirements. You don't want to tell me you love me? Fine. I know how you feel. I can see it on your face and feel it when you kiss me."

She tried again but he shook his head and went on, "You don't do relationships? That's fine, too. We won't have a relationship."

This time he let her talk. "What do you call what we have, then, Jake?"

"Does it matter? It's just us. We can be just us. I don't give a damn what you call it. We're good together. You know it. I know it. Hell, I bet if we asked Sam he'd say we're good together. My parents would agree—I heard what my mother said in the kitchen." He didn't look the least bit guilty for eavesdropping.

No, he looked intense and passionate and loving. As he stroked his finger down the side of her face she knew she had one foot on solid ground and the other on a slippery slope. She tried to get back in control, at least of her own feelings. She started, "I know how good we are together and I know how you feel about me. I even think I know how I feel about you. I don't know if I should…if I can…" There was a long pause while she tried to get her head wrapped around the idea of saying the words she'd never said to any man. She tried. "Jake, I…" The rest of the words didn't want to come out.

He held her closer. "I know, baby, I know."

"I don't know if you do."

"Then explain it to me."

"I've worked so damn hard to get where I am, given up so much. Like I said, being a police detective isn't my job—it's who I am. Those guys I work with are not just my colleagues, they're my family, my friends. My whole world. I can't imagine walking away from it, taking a chance on a relationship that may not work out because I can't be who you want me to be."

"I want you to be the woman I see in front of me. The one I love. I'm not asking you to walk away from your work, to give up your life. Just to let me be part of it."

She still didn't know what to say, except, "I don't deserve you, Jake."

"I know. You deserve someone a whole hell of a lot better looking, with an intact body and a mind that hasn't been fucked up with a tour in a war zone. But you got me. And if you think I'm gonna let you go, even though I know you deserve better, you haven't been paying attention to who I am."

"You know that's not what I meant."

"If it wasn't, it should have been. You're a beautiful, accomplished woman who deserves some guy who's, I don't know, a super hero, maybe, or some star athlete."

Danny almost choked laughing. "Yeah, because I look like the kind of woman who falls for comic book characters. And if you think being arm candy for a rich, spoiled athlete is my style, you're the one not paying attention."

He took her chin again and lightly pressed his mouth against hers. "Seriously, all I'm asking is that you give us a chance. Because now that I've got you here, I'm not about to let you go."

"You have me. What're you going to do with me?"

"I'm going to take you to bed and make love to every inch of you. Slowly and sweetly and for a long, long time."

She could feel the slow curl of hot, thick desire blossom in her body at his words. "Oh, I think I'll like that."

•••

Jake's parents had always said they liked the few women he'd brought home to meet them. But until Danny, they'd never fallen for anyone like they had tonight. Hell, if he hadn't been in love with her before now he would have fallen hard himself.

He'd seen the expression on his mother's face when Danny had prayed the blessing with her, had watched his father listen closely to her frustration at what her colleagues faced every day dealing with people with mental illness with few resources other than handcuffs, pepper spray, and jail. He could tell they loved her intensity and her commitment, admired her passion for her job and for getting it right. He thought they might love her almost as much as he did.

Somehow he had to find a way to convince her that being in love wasn't anything to be afraid of. That she wouldn't lose who she was in a relationship with him. That all he wanted to do was love her and it would be good.

But that was long term and right now, long term could wait. Tonight he simply wanted to make love to her.

He turned the sound system on to his favorite Bach cello music. She grinned over at him as he clicked on the bedside lamp. "What, no candles tonight?"

"You want candles? I can get…"

"Jake, I was teasing." She hooked her finger into the belt loop on his pants, pulled him to her, and began to unbutton his shirt.

"Not tonight. It's all about you tonight." He took her hands and kissed the back of them, then let them drop.

"You say that every time. When is it ever for you?"

"It's always for me, baby. Touching you, tasting you, watching you come. That's always all for me." He was headed for taking off her knit top but then she bit her lower lip and licked the spot where her teeth had made a small indentation, on purpose, he was sure. It didn't matter. He couldn't resist, didn't want to wait. He claimed her mouth for what he intended to be a short little kiss before he went back to undressing her. But once his mouth touched hers, he couldn't stop, couldn't rein in the need to have her that had been building in him all evening.

Instead of the soft, tender kisses he'd thought they'd spend time exchanging, what he was giving her now was hot, hard, and unforgiving. In seconds he knew that her lips weren't enough. He needed to feel her tongue, feel the soft slide of it against his. Feel her body against his, every soft inch of her against every hard inch of him. He gripped the curve of her hips and ground himself against her.

She didn't object. Instead, she twined her arms around his neck and, moaning softly, her body arched against him, she whispered, "I want you. Now."

There was no leisurely, sexy undressing. He stripped off her top, threw it to the floor, and added her bra, pants, and panties in seconds. After he led her to the bed and she crawled in, his clothes were in the pile even faster. He didn't think he'd ever shed his clothes that fast.

She stretched out her arms to him and he lay down beside her. At the same time he took one breast in his mouth, she threw her leg over his hip. Suckling her nipple, pulling at it with his mouth, grazing his teeth over it, he heard her groan deep in her throat, felt her hips rock against his.

Moving to the other breast, he gave it the same attention, drawing back only once to see her face, to watch as she moaned, her eyes fluttering, as she almost came to climax. But he stopped before she got there.

"Please, Jake," she pleaded as he released her breast.

"Soon, baby. Soon," he murmured and began to kiss his way to the delta of now-damp curls at the apex of her thighs. When he got there, she spread her legs to give him access and, making love to her with his mouth, he finished giving her what she wanted, what he had started with her breasts. He circled her clitoris with his tongue and gently scraped his teeth across her most sensitive place, until he could feel her bucking her hips hard against him. Then he licked and sucked until she came apart against him, crying out his name.

Moving back up her body, he settled between her thighs, his now-rock-hard penis up against her sex.

But suddenly he remembered—"Shit. Condom." He rolled over to open the drawer and fumbled around until he found one. He handed it to her and together they ripped the packet open, she unrolled the condom over him and pulled him back between her legs.

In one powerful thrust he was inside her. She was ready for him, wanting him there as much as he wanted to be there. Where he would stay forever if he could. She moved under him in perfect rhythm with him until, finally, he felt her quiver, felt her begin to clench around him and then felt her explode again. Kissing her, plunging his tongue into her mouth with the same power as he thrust his penis into her, he poured himself into her and found his own release.

It took a few minutes for them to regain enough control over their breathing so they could talk. She got there first.

"So, what happened to slow and sweet and for a long, long time?"

He pulled back from her and frowned. "Is that a complaint?"

"Hell, no. Just wondering what caused the changeup."

He kissed her on the end of her nose. "You did, baby. You're the reason. I can't keep my hands off you or my dick out of you."

She burst into laughter. "Mr. Romance certainly disappeared in a hurry."

"I'll go see if I can find him," Jake said as he left to get rid of the condom.

•••

Danny was actually happy he had been so urgent, so demanding in his lovemaking. Urgent sex she could handle tonight. Slow, sweet, and tender she might have had a hard time with.

Any more emotion and she was afraid she'd break into tears, something she hadn't done in years. She didn't cry. Ever. Yet tonight, a couple times she'd felt tears well up in her eyes.

She'd thought she'd gotten over the need for the kind of family connections she'd experienced at dinner tonight. All she needed was her family at work, she'd always told herself, the people who understood her choices, her life. Had she been wrong? Or was she creating this fantasy that could never be as good as she imagined, for reasons she didn't really want to think about?

Before she could explore the idea too much further, Jake came back to bed.

Plenty of time to think about it tomorrow, she thought. *Me and Scarlett O'Hara.* She spooned around him and drifted off to sleep, where she dreamed she was dressed in a hoop-skirted sprigged muslin dress, fending off marauding soldiers with her Glock while Jake took care of the men she wounded.

Chapter Thirteen

"I don't have to ask. I can see how good the weekend was." Sam handed her a cappuccino and grinned. "So, this thing with the doc getting serious?" He acted like treating her to her favorite coffee gave him permission to pry.

"Good weekend. None of your damn business," she said, the growl underlying her response an attempt to ward off any further intrusion into her personal life.

"Of course it's my business. This is how we bond, partner."

"If we haven't bonded in the last three years over a shitload of dead bodies, it ain't gonna happen over my love life."

He sat on the edge of her desk and took a sip of his coffee. "Interesting. You called it your love life, not your sex life."

"Go away, Sam." She busied herself shuffling papers, not really knowing what they were, in an attempt to get the message across that the conversation was over.

"Not talking, huh? Another sign. But I'll leave you alone. For now." He slid off her desk and started to leave. "Oh, wait, Amanda asked me to double check and make sure this Saturday is still on."

"Dinner at your house is fine with Jake. I think he's astounded that not only one but two women were foolish enough to marry you. He'd like to meet the current one."

Sam ignored the dig. "I have the boys this weekend so you might warn him that he'll be socializing with a teenager who occasionally sulks, a toddler who won't shut up, and a middle schooler who tells bad jokes. Oh, and then there's Chihuly. Does he like dogs?"

She laughed. "He'll be fine. And I'll be happy to see your kids."

Their social lives for the weekend taken care of, Sam and Danny turned to less easily settled matters.

The transient camp cases were still not any closer to being cleared. They'd followed up every lead from their interviews with the staff at Veterans Medical Service Clinic but had drawn blanks. No one had noticed any unusual interest in the cardboard boxes from East State Medical Supplies, Inc., although several staff members admitted it was not only possible that their clients swiped cardboard from their recycling, it was probable. The locked gate and razor wire may have kept people out of the alley but it was easy enough to pick up the boxes before they got out there—they were in almost every examining room. And they were a convenient size for their clients to use for storing their belongings. In fact, numerous members of the staff took them for that reason, too. The boxes were sturdy and great for packing or moving.

No one would hazard a guess as to why Jake's patients were being targeted. He was well liked and everyone admired his dedication to the clinic. It made no sense to anyone.

The two detectives had worked through the list of former staff and volunteers, talking to them all with the exception of two who had left the state. Every single avenue led to a dead end.

For Danny, the most troubling loose end was Kaylea's continued absence. She and Sam had looked for her. They tried tracking the cell phone Danny and Jake had given her. It had apparently been destroyed or damaged in some way because there was no trace of it. Jake had searched every place he knew where the homeless vets gathered, slept, or ate. There was no sign of her or of Bob Aronson, her protector from the Forest Park camp.

Then a few weeks after she disappeared, Danny got a phone call, which came, according to caller ID, from Kaylea's phone.

"Kaylea? Where are you? We've been looking for you," Danny said as soon as she saw the number appear on her phone.

There was no response.

"Are you there?"

Nothing.

"Kaylea, do you need help?"

Suddenly there was an odd, rustling noise. Danny thought it might be the sound of the phone being put under something like a blanket or stuffed into a pocket. Without saying anything more, she ended the call.

"Sam, let's try tracking Kaylea's phone again. I think it's been turned back on for us."

Less than twenty minutes later they had the location. She—or at least the phone she'd had—was back in Forest Park.

Sam insisted that if they were headed to that camp they would wear vests and take their Glocks. Although Danny didn't want to appear threatening to Kaylea, she knew he was right—if it was Kaylea who'd called and she was too scared to talk on the phone, something was wrong. And walking into that place when something wasn't right without protection and a weapon was plain reckless.

When they arrived at the trailhead parking lot, Jake Abrams was getting out of his vehicle. Surprised, Danny walked over to him. "What're you doing here?"

He bent down and kissed her cheek. "I'm making rounds. What're you doing?"

Sam joined them. "We got a call from that phone Kaylea Garwood had and it was traced here. We're going to go look for her. How about you join us in the hunt?"

Danny gave her partner a quizzical look, not sure having Jake along was the best idea. But she didn't voice her doubts. At least Jake could save them some time by taking them directly to the camp instead of having her lead Sam in what would probably be a more meandering path there.

Jake took the lead in the hike toward the camp. But as soon as they heard voices that indicated they were close to their destination, Danny went in front of him, with Sam bringing up the rear, both detectives with weapons drawn. Danny could hear a variety of male voices, some of them quite loud, in what sounded like an argument. She couldn't tell what they were arguing about but it was heated and escalating.

They reached the edge of the camp and saw what was, presumably, the source of the disagreement—in the middle of the camp were two men on the ground, piled on top of each other. There was blood on the head and shoulders of the one on top, the one who was not moving. The other man underneath, groaned, as if in pain, and moved fitfully. Around the two downed men was a collection of about ten others, arguing. Kaylea was nowhere in sight.

As soon as Danny was spotted, one of the campers said in a loud voice, "Shit. Who called the cops? I thought we didn't want them here." The shouter glared at the others around him but no one answered. They seemed more interested in moving quickly to the edges of the camp, away from the approaching police.

Before Danny could move to stop them, or ask them what was going on, she saw, on the far side of the camp, a wiry figure dressed head to toe in black, from running shoes to Balaclava face mask, pop out of what Danny recognized as Kaylea's shelter, dragging Kaylea by the feet. The men around the fire pit seemed as startled as Danny was. It was hard to tell much about who the person in black was but it wasn't hard to see that the person was armed—a large, wicked looking, semi-automatic handgun was pointed at Kaylea.

Danny yelled, "Police. Drop the gun and let go of the woman." As soon as she spoke, the group in the center of the camp disappeared into the surrounding trees, leaving a clear path between Danny and the two people across the camp from her.

With the attention of the man in black diverted by the oncoming trio, Kaylea was able to kick her way free. "I'm okay, Danny," she called. "I'm free."

"Now the gun," Danny yelled. "Drop it."

Instead, the shooter raised the pistol. Calling to Sam, "I've got the shot," Danny took a stance to fire but before she could squeeze the trigger, found herself face down in the dirt with a heavy weight crushing her from the back.

She heard the sound of a gunshot from behind her as she tried to get out from under whatever—whoever—was on top of her. She finally wriggled out, sat up, and looked around for her target. He was sprinting into the nearby woods, out of range of her weapon, with Sam in pursuit. Prepared to give one of the transients hell for what they'd done, she turned to see who'd tackled her.

It wasn't one of the campers. It was Jake.

"What the fuck? Why did you do that? I had the shot." She was furious and made no attempt to hide it.

"He was going to shoot you. I had to do something to protect you."

"Protect me? I was doing my job and you interfered." After she wiped the wet dirt off her pants and the sleeves of her shirt, she picked up her weapon. "Goddammit, Jake. Because of you we probably lost him."

Sam returned, winded and even more pissed than Danny was. "Christ, Doc. You really fucked this up. You know we could arrest you for interfering with a police officer doing her duty, don't you? What the hell were you thinking?"

"He was going to shoot Danny," Jake repeated. "I couldn't let that happen."

"First, she had a clean shot at the guy. Second, she's wearing a vest and is a helluva shot. Third, you had no business interfering. Fourth, that guy's gonna keep shooting your patients until we catch him and you just fucked up the best chance we've had to do that." He wiped his hand over his face in frustration. "You happy about that?"

Jake didn't back down. "I wasn't going to stand by and let him shoot Danny when I could prevent it. So I did what had to be done."

"No," Danny said. "You did what you had no business doing." She put her weapon back in her shoulder holster. "Go take a look at those two guys on the ground. One looks like he might be dead, but the other's alive. You take care of your business and let us take care of ours." She knew she sounded cold but it was the only way she could control the hotter-than-hell fury she was feeling.

Before he could respond, she walked through the camp to see how Kaylea was. Danny found her in her shelter where she'd gone after she'd escaped from the man in black.

After she determined Kaylea was all right, Danny asked her what happened. The story Kaylea told confirmed what Danny had suspected—the woman had been scared into silence. She wasn't positive who the killer was, as Danny had thought, but after the last time she'd seen him, she realized there was something about the eyes—the perp's only visible feature—that Kaylea knew was familiar. It was only an impression. She couldn't remember exactly what it was but there was something playing at the edges of her mind that said she'd recognize the killer if she saw him without the Balaclava on.

She'd told Bob Aronson she wanted to disappear and asked for his assistance. He'd made her take the battery out of the phone so they couldn't trace her and he helped her move. In fact, they'd moved three times in the past ten days, trying to keep out of the way of the killer, the police, and Jake Abrams.

Coming back to Forest Park had been his idea, not hers. She was nervous about being there. But things had seemed okay. Until that morning when Kaylea had seen someone dressed all in black hanging around the forest on the outskirts of the camp.

He seemed to be waiting. She didn't have to wonder what it meant. Someone was about to get shot and Kaylea was afraid it was her. But she figured he was biding his time until it got dark before he made his move.

So she dug out the battery, put it back in the phone, and made the call to Danny. But when the detective answered, Kaylea heard someone outside her shelter. She didn't think it was the guy in black but she didn't feel safe talking so she hid the phone in her pocket, keeping it on in hopes that Danny would trace it and get to the camp before the battery power was gone or anyone else got hurt.

But the guy didn't wait. Not too long after she made the call, once again Kaylea heard a rustling noise outside her shelter, this time closer. She pulled out her broken bottle and waited, wondering where her friend Bob was, wondering if she was going to be the next victim, like the message on her shelter had said.

Nothing happened.

Thinking maybe she'd been too anxious, she peeked out of her shelter, wondering if the noise had been made by some animal.

It was some animal—a human one. The guy dressed in black stood in the middle of the camp. He wasn't very tall, shorter than Danny, and skinny but he moved like an athlete. As Kaylea watched he began to turn in a circle and fire indiscriminately in the air. After the first volley of shots there was chaos, of course. But it accomplished what the shooter wanted—as everyone ran to get out of the line of fire, he took aim at one specific person and fired. Apparently, someone got in the way because there was another round of gunshots and then two men down in the center of the encampment, one of them slumped over the other by the fire pit.

After the second man was shot, the shooter ran to Kaylea's shelter. He never spoke to her, only threatened her by waving the gun. When she resisted following him outside, he hit her with the gun, knocked her down, and dragged her out by the feet.

The rest Danny knew.

When Kaylea finished her story, Danny said, "Kaylea, now will you come in with us and let us find you a safe place to stay? Please?"

Tears welled up in the other woman's eyes. "I can't live inside a little room. I can't. Besides, if I go someplace where he knows the social service puts people like me, he'll track me there. Please, Danny. Let Bob take care of me. We'll disappear again. But this time I'll keep in touch with you. I promise."

Danny scraped her hands over her face in a gesture she realized was exactly like the one her partner used when he was frustrated. "I can't force you to come in, although I have a good mind to put you in protective custody."

Kaylea shuddered. "Jail? Please, no. I'd go crazy."

Danny stared at the terrified woman for a long moment, a solution to the problem beginning to occur to her. "I have an idea. If you won't let me find you a bed in an SRO, would you come home with me?"

"You mean to your house?"

"Yeah. I have a guest room. You'd have to share a bathroom with me but you'd have your own room and a place to, I don't know, watch TV or read or something, where you'd be safe. You could stay there until we find a place for you. An apartment, maybe. Not just a bed or a small room."

"Why would you do something like that?"

"Because you're in danger and I need you safe until this is over. And I very much doubt this guy will track you to my house."

Kaylea stared at her, chewing her lip for a long time before saying softly, "Let me talk to Bob."

"Okay. While you do that, I'll go take care of some personal business of my own."

Danny ducked out of the shelter and scanned the camp. Sam was talking to a couple of the campers. Two uniformed officers and a couple EMTs were working the scene, too, in response, she assumed, to a call from her partner. It was apparent from the reduced number of men standing around the shelters and tents that some of their witnesses had disappeared into the woods before anyone had a chance to stop them. And she was certain they wouldn't willingly reappear to talk to a bunch of cops. She wasn't sure she could blame them. Talking to the cops hadn't helped get this guy shut down. They must've felt they were better off disappearing into the wilderness park.

The person she was looking for wasn't immediately apparent either. Then, from behind her, she heard his familiar voice.

"Am I forgiven?" For the first time since she'd met him, Jake sounded unsure of himself.

She faced him. "Forgiven? For what you did? Hell, no. How would you like it if I burst into your surgery and threw myself on you so you couldn't operate because I was afraid the patient had HIV and you might catch it by operating on them?"

"That's absurd. We do all sorts of tests and take every possible precaution against something like that happening. I'm perfectly safe."

"Right. Like we train for potentially dangerous situations and take every possible precaution to make sure we're safe. You had no right—you had no business—doing what you did, any more than I have the right to interfere with what you do in your job."

He tried to put his hand on her shoulder but she shrugged it off. "No, Jake, you're not going to cuddle or kiss or caress your way out of this." She stepped back out of his reach. "I've told you every way I know how that you can't dictate to me how I do my job. But apparently I wasn't clear enough. So let me be now: What you did today is unacceptable. I won't tolerate it. Ever. Under any circumstances. Do you understand?"

She could see his anger building by the set of his shoulders and the thinning line of his mouth. He looked like he did the first time she'd seen him, when he was angry about the death of Jim

Branson. "I don't give a damn what you say. If I had it to do over, I would. I won't stand by and watch the same thing happen to someone I love that happened to the guys in Iraq."

"We're in Portland, not in a war zone."

"It sure as hell looks like a war zone to me. How many more dead and wounded does it take for you to qualify it as one?"

"It's a crime scene and I'm a cop. This is what I do. And you cannot—I won't let you—keep me from doing my work."

"It's just a damn job."

"Maybe that's the problem. Maybe what you don't understand is what else I've been trying to tell you. This isn't a damn job to me. It's who I am. If you can't accept that…"

She stopped, knowing that what they said next would be either the beginning of a new phase of what was between them or the end of it.

"Suppose I can't accept it," he said, his voice low and strained.

"If you can't accept who I am, then we can't be together." She walked away without looking back.

She threw herself into getting the crime scene details taken care of. Sam didn't need a prompt to take over the job of interviewing and handling Jake. He just did it. Before the doctor left, he made a move to come talk to Danny but she fended it off by getting into a conversation with one of the other cops. By the time they'd finished talking, Jake was headed out to the parking lot.

The only good thing that happened was that Kaylea agreed to come stay with her until Danny found a suitable place for her to live. Danny wasn't sure whether her relief at that decision was solely because of her fears for Kaylea's safety or because she knew that having a roommate, even for a short time, would help take her mind off the gaping hole that had been torn in her gut when she'd seen Jake Abrams walking alone down the trail toward his vehicle. Without looking back.

Chapter Fourteen

It took her a couple of days but finally Danny made a phone call she knew she had to make. Amanda picked up on the second ring.

"Danny, I'm so glad to hear from you. I've wanted to check on you but Sam asked me to wait until you called. How're you doing?"

"I'm okay. Not the best week I've ever had but I'll get over it. So, you know that dinner on Saturday is off, then."

"It doesn't have to be. The three of us can…"

"I guess Sam didn't tell you this part but I have a temporary house guest, one of the vets from the Forest Park camp. She needed a safe place to stay until we get her settled, so she's with me."

"No, he didn't tell me. But she's welcome, too."

"I doubt she'd feel comfortable, Amanda. It took her forever to warm up to me. Besides, I don't think I'm ready to be social yet. Kaylea—the woman staying with me—is about all the company I can handle."

"I understand. But you know the invitation is always open for you, don't you?"

"Of course I do. Thanks for understanding."

She was about to end the call when Amanda said, "Danny, did Sam ever tell you why his first marriage broke up?"

Surprised, she said, "No. Other than his sons, he never really talks about that part of his life."

"Well, I don't think I'm betraying any great secret but you might want to know the story." She waited for a moment and when Danny didn't say anything, continued. "When Sam and his first wife got married, he was a middle manager for an electric utility."

"I didn't know that."

"Not many people in the Bureau do. Thing is, he was bored and looking for another career option when one night at a dinner party, he met the husband of one of his wife's colleagues—she's a school teacher…"

"That I did know. Middle school, right?"

"Yup, where they should get combat pay. Anyway, Sam's bored, meets this guy who's a cop and gets interested. He applies, is accepted, and goes through the Academy. Six months into his rookie year, his partner gets shot. Not killed. Not even badly hurt. But it scared the hell out of Sam's wife. They'd just had a second baby and she was sure she was going to end up a widow."

"Oh, crap."

"He offered to quit but she wouldn't let him. He was clearly happier than he'd been at his old job so she tried to tough it out for a year or two but she couldn't. They divorced. Not too long after she marries a guy who's got a nice, safe desk job and a year or so after that Sam and I meet."

"So, the moral of your story is…?"

"There's no moral, Danny. I only wanted you to know your partner knows exactly, and I mean exactly, what you're going through. He may pretend otherwise but he's an old softie when it comes to people he cares about. And he's worried about you. Don't wall yourself off from people who are concerned about you."

Danny gulped back the lump in her throat. "I didn't think I was but maybe you're right. Maybe I should…I don't know…talk to someone. It's been killing me. I miss Jake so much but I can't stop being who I am to be with him. I don't know what to do."

"You're smart. You're resourceful. You'll figure it out."

• • •

Jake hadn't slept well in days. The dreams had come back. Not as bad as they had been when he first returned from Iraq but bad enough. Finally he'd called the psychiatrist who'd worked with him four years before and made an appointment. The shrink told him he thought what had happened in Forest Park had triggered an attack of PTSD. Jake wasn't sure that's what it was. He'd managed it so well for the past few years that he was more inclined to think it was a legitimate worry about the woman he loved and how she put herself in harm's way. That was reasonable. PTSD wasn't.

Whoever was right, when the dreams didn't stop he had to acknowledge there was some relation to his experience in Iraq. And it was losing him yet another woman. The loss of his almost-fiancée paled into insignificance when compared to this. Danny was the real deal, the woman he knew he wanted to be with for the rest of his life.

So that meant he had to figure a way around it. He wasn't about to give up, not this time.

This was more damage than flowers and chocolate could repair, he knew that. He and Danny had to work it out, find a way to deal with his anxiety and her job. To do that, she'd have to talk to him and that wasn't happening. She wouldn't respond to any of his attempts to communicate. He was desperate enough to try texting and emailing even though he knew that was hardly personal enough. But she didn't answer those messages any more than she'd responded to the phone messages he'd left her. Nothing worked.

He thought about waiting for her outside Central Precinct and trying to convince her she should talk to him, even waited in the park across the street once when he was on his way to make rounds at the camps close to the time she usually went into work. But when he saw her, he didn't move to intercept her. He wasn't sure she'd stop long enough for him to say anything and he didn't want to make a scene.

Then he decided he'd wait for her at her house. On his second evening vigil of waiting and wondering where the hell she was, it occurred to him that one of her neighbors might have warned her about him sitting there and it would look like he was stalking her. Which, of course, he was. That would likely get a restraining order out against him, seriously affecting his chances of explaining it all to her. So he gave up on the idea of trying to hunt her down there, too.

Then he had an idea—he'd talk to Sam. If anyone knew her, he did. Maybe he'd have some good advice.

So, instead of continuing to stalk Danny, he began to stalk Sam.

Off and on for three days, mostly at lunchtime or when he thought Sam might be leaving for home, Jake sat in the rain across from the Justice Center and watched for him to come in or out of Central Precinct. No luck. Finally on day four, the sun came out and so did Sam. Jake followed him to a food cart, watched as he ordered his lunch, then approached him.

"Sam, can I talk to you for a minute?"

"I wondered when you'd make your move. You've been stalking me long enough. Sure, Doc. If you don't mind my eating in front of you, we can go over to that bench. I have about fifteen minutes before I have to be at a meeting."

When they were settled, Jake began, "What I wanted to talk to you about was…" He was suddenly short of words, not able to put a coherent sentence together.

Sam swallowed the bite of gyros he had in his mouth before rescuing him. "Let me see if I can help. You know you fucked up big time in Forest Park and you're trying to figure a way to get to my partner so you can explain yourself because you've decided you can't live without her or something like that. That cover it?"

"Thanks, yeah. I know I have to apologize for what I did, tell her I'm sorry, but…"

"*Are* you sorry for what you did? Or are you sorry it drove her away and you'll say whatever it takes to get her back?"

"You're good at your job, too, aren't you?"

"Good, *too*? Meaning, you're good at your job or she's good at hers?"

"Holy hell, Sam. Remind me never to get crosswise with you. I wouldn't like the interrogation."

"So, let's agree that we're all good at what we do—you, me, Danny—and move on. Answer the questions about being sorry."

"I don't know the answer to your question about being sorry for what I did. I'm still working that out. I know I'm dead sorry I drove her away. But I don't know yet if I can say I wouldn't do the same thing if the situation occurred again."

Sam took another bite of the gyros, carefully pulling down the paper it was wrapped in, a thoughtful look on his face while he chewed and stared at Jake. "What'd your shrink say about this?"

"How do you know I talked to my psychiatrist?"

He ignored the question. "What'd he...she...say?"

"He says I reacted instinctively, like I would have in Iraq. He said it's not necessarily related to Danny. I'm not so sure." He took a deep breath and asked the question he most needed an answer to. "How's your wife handle what you do?"

"The first one left me because she couldn't live with it. Amanda trusts that I know what I'm doing." He polished off his lunch and wiped his fingers on a napkin before balling the trash up in a neat package and standing up.

"She knows that, statistically, I'm more likely to be hurt in a car accident driving to work than I am on duty. And she knows I don't take unnecessary risks. She trusts me, like I trust her to take safety precautions in her glass studio so she doesn't inhale powdered glass and ruin her lungs or slash a major blood vessel open by carelessly handling one of the big sheets of glass she works with every day. We trust each other. It's what people who love each other do, Jake."

Jake stood up, not sure what to say next. So he did the only thing he could think to do—he put out his hand and said, "Thanks, Sam. I appreciate you talking to me."

Sam took his hand. "Not a problem." He pitched his trash into a nearby container then added, "One more thing—about getting caught crosswise with me? You'd really hate it if you got there by making my partner any more unhappy than you already have." He ambled away, leaving Jake with no idea how any of what Sam had told him would get him closer to Danny but unaccountably happy to know that she was unhappy right now, too.

Chapter Fifteen

"Doctor Abrams, there was a phone call for you a few minutes ago." Barbara Black, who was temporarily staffing the front desk, said.

Following his conversation with Sam, Jake had made rounds at the hospital and had pre-op visits with the patients he was operating on the next day. He was tired, he was out of sorts, and he wasn't sure he should even be at the clinic.

What he was sure of was he didn't know what had just been said to him. "Sorry, Barbara, I wasn't listening carefully. Who did you say called?" The office manager wasn't his favorite staff member and he knew she returned the feeling. He didn't like the patronizing tone she used for their patients. She didn't like the way the patients turned to him with questions about the clinic. Some of them were spooked by her and her different colored eyes—one was blue, the other hazel—that gave her an off kilter look.

"You got a phone call from someone named Kaylea. She said she needed to see you and you'd know where she was."

Kaylea called him here? What the fuck? "Did she say why she needed to see me?"

"No, but she sounded pretty upset. She was whispering. Like she didn't want someone to hear her. Is she one of your patients?"

"Yeah, she has been." He looked around at the full waiting room. *Shit, he couldn't leave now. Not with this many people waiting to be seen.* "Is there another doctor here right now, Barbara, to help Doctor Campbell?"

"Doctor Nelson should be here any minute."

He looked at the clock. It was almost five. "I hate to do this but I need to go see what Kaylea wants. I'll be back as soon as I can. I'll tell Tom Campbell before I leave."

"I'll tell him. I'm on my way to the back to get my coat and go home anyway. You get going."

"That's okay, Barbara. I'll take care of it. Thanks for getting the message to me."

• • •

Jake knew Kaylea was Danny's temporary roommate, although he didn't think Danny was aware Bob Aronson had told him. That made him a little uneasy about going to her house when, he assumed, she wasn't there but he didn't think Kaylea would have contacted him had she not been in trouble. The thought crossed his mind that he should call Kaylea to find out what he was walking into but if she'd been whispering, afraid someone would hear her, he didn't want to alert whoever that was.

He even thought about calling Danny but he dismissed that idea, too, assuming that if Kaylea had wanted Danny, she would have called her.

Arriving at Danny's house, he sat at the curb, looking around, trying to see if he recognized a car, a person, anything that looked suspicious. It was difficult to be sure in the darkening evening but he didn't think he saw anyone who looked familiar, nor did he see a small, dark colored sedan like the one described by some of the witnesses to the shootings.

There was a light on in Danny's living room, but that was the only sign of life in the apartment. After Jake's recon of the street from inside the car, he got out and walked the block, doing a quick sweep of it from the sidewalk. Still nothing.

He approached the house, all his senses on high alert.

Kaylea didn't answer the door when he rang the bell. When he knocked and called her name he finally got a response. A weak, scared-sounding voice asked, "Who is it?"

"It's me, Kaylea. Jake Abrams. You called the clinic and said you wanted to see me."

"I didn't call Doctor Abrams. I don't know who you are but whoever you are, you're lying."

"Kaylea, look through the peephole in Danny's door. You'll see it's me."

There was silence, presumably while she checked him out. Then, as he heard the clink of a security chain being undone and the thunk of a deadlock being released, she said, "It is you. But I didn't…"

Kaylea was interrupted by someone behind Jake speaking, the voice somehow familiar. "That's right. You didn't call him, Kaylea. But it was the only way I knew how to get us all together like one big happy family."

Before he could turn to see who it was, Kaylea said, "Oh, fuck, Doctor Abrams. That's him…her. Those eyes. Now I know. That's who shot up the camp."

The person behind him shoved a weapon into Jake's back. "Inside, Doctor Know-It-All. Get inside now."

• • •

Danny finally had a lead on the car seen at the camps. After running the various possible combinations of partial license plates through the DMV database, she had a list of small, dark colored sedans in the Portland area. She'd worked her way through it, cross-referencing it with the staff and volunteer list at VMSC. Sure enough, a black Honda sedan belonged to someone there. Not a man, but the officer manager, a woman named Barbara Black.

Danny headed for Old Town and the clinic.

What she discovered there made her very uneasy. Greta was at the front desk and told her that Jake had come in for his shift about ten minutes before and almost immediately left. The doctor who'd talked to Jake said he'd been called out for a patient named Kay Leese, or something like that, who'd asked for help.

It didn't take much of a mental leap to get from Kay Leese to Kaylea. But why had she called Jake at the clinic? She didn't have that number on her cell phone. She had Danny's and Jake's cell phone numbers. Why hadn't she called one of them?

When Danny asked to speak to the person who'd taken the message, the news got worse. Barbara Black, who'd been covering for Greta while she took a coffee break, had given him the message. But Barbara wasn't around. She'd left shortly after Jake had, saying she needed to go home early because of a family emergency.

Shit. Shit. Shit.

Danny ran to her car and headed over the river, calling Sam while she was crossing the Broadway Bridge and filling him in on what was happening. He would take care of backup. But she was going to be the first person on scene and she had to figure out how they were going to handle it.

She cruised the street, scoping it out. What she saw confirmed her worst fears. Parked directly in front of her house was Jake's SUV. Parked three cars behind it was a black Honda sedan, license plate 639 MLS.

Quadruple shit. Kaylea and Jake were inside Danny's home with the person who had just rocketed to the top of Danny's suspect list as the murderer of four people.

Danny parked her car around the corner from her house and assessed the situation. She had no idea where Barbara, Jake, and Kaylea were in the apartment so she wasn't sure whether she and her team should go in the front or the back. They didn't want to put Jake and Kaylea in any more danger than they already were.

She decided to scope out the front of the house while she waited for Sam and her backup. She felt confident she could do that without being seen. The evening was dark and cloudy, the moon barely visible. Added to that, she was in a black raincoat and dark pants which would help her blend into the night. For the first time in weeks she was grateful the streetlight outside her house was out. She'd been making phone calls all over hell and half of Georgia to get it replaced but right now she was happy she'd been so ineffective in eliciting a response.

Stashing her Glock in her leather case, she got out of her car. Nothing seemed out of the ordinary; nothing was visible through her front window. She was about to go back to her car to wait for Sam when she heard what sounded like a gunshot coming from inside her house.

Waiting for backup was now out of the question.

The outside light, the one beside the door, wasn't on, which was good. There was a single light on in the living room, the one on a timer set to turn on at four. That gave her light when she came in the house after work but because it was on a table in the front window, the glare made it almost impossible to see beyond it to anything else in the room. That was bad. She was walking almost blind into what surely was a setup.

She removed the Glock from her leather case, chambered a round and entered the house, leaving the front door unlocked.

"Kaylea?" she called. "I heard a noise that sounded like a gunshot? Are you okay?"

No response.

Before she turned out the light in the living room, she looked around. Nothing looked out of place. There was no sign of a struggle. There was no other light on any place in the house except for a dim glow coming from the kitchen.

She called again, "Kaylea? Where are you?"

An unfamiliar woman's voice came from the back of the house. "You're home early. I expected to be gone by the time you got here, Detective Hartmann. You've surprised me and I don't like surprises."

"Who are you and where's Kaylea? What are you doing in my home?" Danny took a few steps further into the house now that she knew where Barbara Black was.

"Kaylea can't talk to you right now, I'm afraid." The voice was getting closer. "And who am I? I'm the person who's going to stop all this interference in my work."

Finally, a slim, boyish figure wearing surgical gloves and with her hair covered with a surgical cap appeared in the door from the kitchen to the dining room. She was holding the arm of a bound and gagged Kaylea. Because she was backlit by the kitchen light, Danny couldn't see Barbara Black's face but the gun pointed at Kaylea's head was only too obvious.

"I'm sorry," Danny said. "I can't see you. Have we met?"

"We sure as hell have, at the clinic I run." Barbara walked two more steps into the dining room and turned on the overhead light. "The gun. Put it on the table. Over here, where I can reach it. Then walk away from it."

Danny hesitated for a few seconds, trying to figure out how to keep her Glock without causing the woman in front of her to hurt Kaylea.

"Put. It. Down." Barbara motioned with the gun she held.

Danny did as the woman demanded. "Now I recognize you. Barbara, isn't it? Barbara Black. You're the office manager at VMSC."

Barbara picked up Danny's Glock and tucked it into the waistband of her pants. "I'm surprised you remembered. You certainly didn't pay much attention to me when you were there in spite of the fact I'm the person who makes sure the clinic is run right. You should have talked to me first. But you didn't. You were too busy flaunting yourself in front of that son-of-a-bitch doctor who tortures patients."

"I don't understand." Danny took a step forward but was met by Barbara matching her move, blocking her. "Do you mean Doctor Abrams?"

"Stay put, missy." Barbara waved the gun around. "Of course that's who I mean. Don't play games with me."

Danny edged around the dining room table, an inch at a time. "Are you okay, Kaylea?

Kaylea nodded and tried to shake off Barbara's hand. Barbara tightened her grip and pulled her hostage back into the kitchen without taking her eyes off Danny.

Without asking permission Danny followed and watched Barbara push Kaylea onto a kitchen chair, then stand behind her and tie her to the chair with the cords Danny recognized as coming from the curtains.

Most of the kitchen was in shadow; the only light was from the bulb under the range hood. Danny couldn't see much other than what was right in front of her, couldn't see if Jake was in the room. But she noticed a peculiar, almost metallic, smell. It was recognizable and yet somehow out of place. Like she knew it from somewhere else, someplace familiar.

Then Barbara flipped on the overhead light and Danny saw what the source of the smell was. It was familiar, all right. She'd seen it at too many crime scenes.

Blood.

Chapter Sixteen

Blood was in puddles in several places on the floor, apparently dribbled down from the corner of the counter next to the sink; the sharp corner, where the ceramic tile had a jagged edge she'd never gotten around to having her landlord repair. She scanned Kaylea looking for evidence of a wound but saw none. Then she turned toward the pantry and almost threw up.

The source of the blood was lying in a crumbled heap on the floor—Jake, with more blood on his face, neck, and shoulders. She couldn't tell if he was alive or dead but from the amount of blood she feared it was the latter.

She looked away quickly, afraid to let Barbara see it distressed her. "Barbara, can we take that towel off Kaylea's mouth? It must be irritating her."

"I really don't care. She won't be around long enough to have her mouth irritated." She had a smirk on her face again. "I'd have thought you were more concerned about your boyfriend than about her."

"I'm afraid you misinterpreted our relationship, Barbara. He's not my boyfriend."

"Well, he thought he was. You should have heard him protecting you by trying to make me leave."

"Can't help what he thought. We had dinner a couple times and that was it." Danny wanted to keep the conversation going while she came up with some way to get to Jake and see if he was still alive. "What happened, Barbara? Did he fall or what?"

"I thought you said he didn't matter to you?"

"I'm a cop. I investigate things like this all the time. What happened?"

"It's not important. The only thing that matters is that he's no longer going to torture those men with his useless therapies and waste our limited resources trying to cure people who can't be cured."

"Torturing patients? We didn't hear anything about that when we talked to the clinic…to your staff."

"Of course not. No one would be brave enough to cross the mighty Doctor Abrams."

"I'm not clear on what you think he did." Danny wanted Barbara talking while she looked around to see what she could use to get control of the situation.

"He made those men go through hell recalling what they'd been through so he could pretend to cure them. You can't cure them. You can only give them drugs and send them home or put them out of their misery. So I did what needed to be done. And I took care of the source of the problem, too. Permanently."

"Jake…Doctor Abrams? So he's…?" Danny couldn't say the word.

"Dead. He's dead. I shot him and he fell and he's dead." Barbara had a twisted, berserk grin on her face as she said three times the word Danny hadn't been able to say once. "Not that it matters. It's only important that he's no longer going to be running things at the clinic. Doctor Burns and I will be back to treating patients the right way."

"Is that what this is about…running the clinic? I thought he was a volunteer there. Don't paid staff members have more say than volunteers?"

"You'd think that would be the way it works. But he," she pointed at Jake with the gun, "he came charging in and took over. I was running things with Doctor Burns until he came along and forced himself on everyone. I should be running the clinic. But no, he flooded the place with those men who can't be cured and took up time and money we needed to treat the really deserving patients."

This was far more than the clash of personalities she and Sam had heard about when they interviewed the clinic staff. How had

Barbara been able to conceal the contempt she felt for Jake? Why hadn't someone—Jake, especially—not seen the depths of this woman's anger? "I can see how that would upset you, Barbara. He was difficult to deal with sometimes, I agree."

Barbara ranted on allowing Danny a chance to look hard at Jake. She swore she saw him breathe but maybe that was her imagination, what she wanted to see. If only she could get to him to see what shape he was in.

Then Kaylea gave her the opportunity she wanted. Freeing one hand from the cords that Barbara had apparently tied too loosely, Kaylea pulled the kitchen towel she had around her mouth off and yanked at the cord holding her to the chair. Barbara ran to her and smacked her across the face. "Sit still, missy. Do as you're told."

Kaylea yelled, "Is Doctor Abrams okay, Danny?"

"Stop it," Barbara said followed by yet another slap.

Danny took the chance, went to the pantry and knelt by Jake.

But Barbara noticed. "You stop, too! This isn't part of my plan. You're messing with my plans. Both of you. Stop now."

"I'm just saying the Kaddish prayer over Jake. We're both Jewish and it's an important thing to do as soon as someone Jewish dies."

Barbara stared at Danny for a few moments until Kaylea struggled against her bonds again and Barbara had to return to her task of retying Kaylea to the chair.

One obstacle overcome, Danny had only two other concerns. First, she didn't know the words to the Kaddish prayers. Second, she wondered if the rabbi who'd tried to engage her interest in her mother's faith would somehow find out the lies she was telling about the religion and hunt her down. She thought it unlikely but you never knew.

One thing she wasn't worried about, if God existed—and was listening—she was sure he'd understand what she was up to.

With her heart beating a dangerously rapid rhythm and her breath catching in her throat, she placed herself so she was blocking Barbara's view of what she was doing and began to speak, slowly and loudly.

She started with what she'd recently prayed with Jake's mother, the Sabbath blessing, which she repeated over and over as she felt Jake's wrist, his temple, the base of his neck for a pulse, her fingers turning red from the blood that seemed to have come from a large gash in his head that lifted a piece of his scalp. She knew head wounds bled profusely and hoped the blood all over the floor was a reflection of that rather than of a life-threatening gunshot wound someplace else.

Whether it was because Jake heard her, or God did, something made him open his eyes at that point. She stumbled on the words she was praying as she saw the first sign he was alive. But she didn't want Barbara to know he was so she shook her head a little and raised her bloody finger in front of his lips. He nodded acquiescence and closed his eyes.

As she praised Adonai as the ruler of the universe more times than she had in the past decade, she found a carotid pulse. It was rapid and not as strong as she thought his normal pulse would be but it was there. Satisfied that he was alive and in reasonably good shape, she began to surreptitiously pat him down, looking for something, anything, she could use against Barbara.

As she searched, she continued to pray, now pulling out of her memory every Hebrew phrase she could remember, the Yiddish her grandparents had used when they were trying to keep the grandkids from knowing what they were talking about, even a couple words she thought might sound vaguely like Hebrew. It all flowed from her mouth like water in the river Jordan.

She swore she saw Jake smiling.

Barbara eventually lost patience with her. "Get it over with. He's dead. Finish. You've upset my plans enough by coming home early. I need you over here where I can see what you're doing while I think.

"I'm almost finished," Danny said. She wasn't sure how Barbara thought she could get away with ridding herself of all three of them but that was Barbara's problem. Hers was trying to find something she could use to help her prevent any more shooting before Sam arrived and found a way in.

One last pass of patting down Jake's pockets and one last iteration of "Baruch atah Adonai" and she was almost ready to stand up when she found his cell phone, in a jeans pocket she'd apparently missed on her first pass. At last, something that might be of help. She hoped Jake had Sam's number programmed in. All she had to do was find it, call it, and make enough noise that Barbara didn't hear him answer.

Right. Not a problem.

Turned out, it wasn't. As if she were on Danny's wavelength, Kaylea suddenly began to moan and scream as loud as she could around the newly reapplied gag. Barbara was forced to tend to her again, giving Danny the chance to find Sam's number, press it, and put the phone beside Jake. She heard her partner answer and when he did she yelled, "Kaylea, are you all right? Barbara, what's wrong with her? Is that gag too tight?"

Sam stopped talking, like she wanted him to do.

Barbara was frantically pacing back and forth between the pantry and the back of the kitchen, between her moaning captive and Danny.

"Stop it. Both of you. I'll shoot you both if you don't shut up."

Danny signaled to Kaylea to be quiet. Then she stood and said, "Thank you, Barbara, for letting me do that."

Barbara barely acknowledged Danny so intent was she on figuring out how to manage two live hostages and one she thought was dead. Apparently she had originally wanted to leave two dead bodies for Danny to find when she got home from work but had to abandon that when Danny arrived home early. Now, she kept muttering about ways to get all three of them someplace where she could "take care of them." For one freaky moment she actually seemed to ask Danny for advice before shaking her head and continuing to talk out with herself the options.

All of which made Danny believe Barbara had been pushed to the limit and was unstable. Which made her very, very dangerous.

Finally Barbara seemed to have decided on a plan. She looked at Danny and said, "I need your help getting him," she pointed with the weapon toward Jake, "in the car. We can carry him between us. And I want her in handcuffs," here she nodded at Kaylea, "so it looks like you're arresting her. That way, we can all leave together. You'll drive. He'll be in the front seat. She'll be handcuffed in the back seat with me." She paused for a moment. "You do have handcuffs, don't you?"

Danny had a hard time not doing some kind of happy dance. There was a carving set in her dining room. If she could get to it, she'd be armed with something. "If I do, they'll be in that leather case I put on the dining room table. I'll go get them."

"No, you stay right where you are. I'll go get them," Barbara said.

Once again Kaylea slipped an arm out of the cording that bound her to the chair and pulled at the towel over her mouth. "Run, Danny. Get help." she yelled.

"Dammit," Barbara screamed. "Stay where you are." Her voice was thin and tense. She gestured again with the gun and said to Danny, "Go get the handcuffs but no messing around in there. Get them and come back here. I'll take care of missy over there." She went to the back of the kitchen and Danny headed for the dining room.

When she got to the other side of the dining room table, Danny pulled out a couple zip ties from her bag and said, in a conversational tone, "Barbara, I don't have handcuffs but I do have plastic zip ties. We use them in place of handcuffs sometimes. Will that work for you?" She stuck two into her pants pocket as she spoke.

Barbara didn't turn to respond. She was concentrating too much on the squirming Kaylea in front of her. Danny nodded at Kaylea who went into another episode of noise making and moving around. Barbara, seemingly frustrated at her inability to control the half-bound woman, put her weapon on the breakfast room table and yanked hard on the restraint, clearly hurting Kaylea with the action.

Danny had started toward the sideboard, where the carving set was, when she heard the soft but distinctive sound of her front door opening and the click of her partner's cowboy boots on the wooden floor in the living room behind her.

She'd never been so glad to hear any sound in her life.

Sam doused the dining room light, came up behind Danny, and whispered, "So, what's the plan, partner?"

Danny whispered back, "No plan. So far, it's been strictly seat-of-the-pants."

"I've trained you well, Grasshopper. Where's your weapon?"

"Barbara has it."

"I take it back. I haven't trained you well enough yet. Good thing one of us is still armed."

"Shut up, Sam. Where's the rest of our backup?"

"A bunch of our friends are outside waiting for me to tell them what to do. But I figured we could take care of this ourselves and let them do the cleanup."

"Then let's get it done."

Motioning him to move to the right-hand side of the door to the kitchen, she went to the left just as Barbara finished re-securing Kaylea. A frown crossed Barbara's face as she looked out into the darkened dining room. Picking up her gun, she walked to the door of the room.

"What's going on out here?" she asked.

Danny and Sam each grabbed an arm and lifted her off the ground and she found out. With a sharp chop to Barbara's right wrist, Danny disarmed her. Without firing a shot they had the situation under control.

While Danny used the zip ties on Barbara, Sam signaled for the rest of the backup team to come in and got the EMTs for Jake. He was marginally conscious as they loaded him onto the gurney and Danny thought he was trying to say something to her. She knew if she went to him she would break down so she concentrated on getting Kaylea untied and onto a second gurney so she, too, could be taken to the hospital.

After both Kaylea and Jake were gone and Barbara was on her way to the Justice Center, Danny collapsed into a dining room chair. "Well, I doubt I'll ever want to cook a meal in there again," she said, nodding toward the kitchen.

"It'll be fine once it's cleaned up. And the doc didn't look too bad when they hauled him out of there. You did good, partner. You kept her talking and engaged until we could get in. You should get a commendation for this."

"Save the awards and decorations for later. I'm just glad it's over and we caught the fucker. Although she wasn't exactly who I thought the fucker would be."

Sam laughed. "Me neither. But I'm not about to tell anyone that. L.T. wants to hear from you…from us. Even if you're not happy with how this all turned out, he will be. Shall I tell him to meet us at the hospital?"

"Yeah, I want to get to the hospital and see how…see how Kaylea is."

"Yeah, you go see how Kaylea is." Sam punched her lightly on the upper arm. "Who you trying to fool, Hartmann, about who you're going to see?"

She sighed. "Me, I guess."

"And how's that working for you?"

"Not well."

Chapter Seventeen

Kaylea and Jake were taken to the same hospital where Sam had been treated when he'd been shot. Now, in a creepy déjà vu, Danny was waiting to see how another gunshot victim was doing.

But the hospital and the injury were all that were similar. The rest was uncomfortable, new territory, like much of her relationship— dammit, her friendship—oh, hell, whatever it was she had—with Jake. It had been professional when she'd been there for Sam, and she'd had Amanda and Margo for backup. Now she was alone and it was way too personal.

Besides, back then she'd been sure of how she'd be received by the patient in question. But Jake? She'd been avoiding him for days, wasn't sure he wanted to see her and was even less sure how she'd feel when she saw him.

Then there was his father. She knew for damn sure she didn't want to face him. And she had a snowball's chance in hell of avoiding him since Danny knew that within minutes of Jake's arrival the entire staff of the hospital would recognize the name and get the news to the senior Doctor Abrams. It was only a matter of time before he showed up in the ER.

Danny went looking for her boss who, she hoped, had arrived. Reporting to him would get her out of the way. Except she couldn't find him or Sam. So she tried to become part of the woodwork, hanging out in the waiting room with her back to the door so if Jake's father came in, he wouldn't notice her.

Of course it didn't work. Harold Abrams saw her as soon as he came into the room and immediately came up behind her, putting his arm around her shoulders. She turned to see a grim faced and tense looking man who, as she'd expected, was clearly reacting as a father to what had happened, not as a doctor.

"Danny, I'm so glad I found you," he said as he hugged her. "I ran into your partner down the hall. He told me you were the one who got Jake out of the mess he was in. I don't know how to begin to thank you."

"Sam and a whole lot of other cops got all of us out," she said, untangling herself from his embrace. "How is he? How's Jake?" She tried to sound calm but could hear the strain in her voice.

"He has a flesh wound in his thigh from a bullet. Apparently he tried to get the weapon away from that woman and the gun went off. He fell, and hit his head on something sharp—he has a large gash in his head. It took I don't even know how many stitches to close it. He doesn't remember too clearly what happened after he fell. He did say he tried to play dead so she wouldn't do any more damage."

An image of how dead Jake looked lying on her pantry floor flashed through Danny's mind and she shuddered. "Yeah, he did a good job at that. Fooled us all."

"I talked to the other woman…his patient…I can't remember her name…"

"Kaylea Garwood."

"Right. Kaylea. She said he fell hard and just lay there. She was convinced he was dead."

Danny needed to get the image of the dead-looking Jake out of her head so she asked, "Do you know how she is? Kaylea, I mean? They insisted she come here to be checked out, too."

"They examined her thoroughly and she's fine. Pretty badly shaken up but physically she's okay. I think they're about ready to release her. I understand she was staying with you. Will you be taking her home with you?"

"I don't think either of us wants to go back there right now. I need to get someone in to clean up all the…clean up…get the kitchen…" The image of Jake bleeding all over her floor was back again.

"It's okay, Danny. I know how head wounds bleed. It must have made a mess." He put his arm around her shoulder again. "Do you have a place to stay? You and your houseguest are welcome to come stay with us."

"No, thank you. I've already made other arrangements." She hadn't and she was sure Harold Abrams knew she hadn't but she was not about to go stay with Jake's parents. That would only pull her deeper into the quicksand of Abrams family life, which couldn't happen. Not when things with Jake were like they were and a solution to their problems was nowhere in sight.

"Well, then I'll let you go check on Jake and then you and… Kaylea? Is that her name? Good heavens, I can't keep anything in my head for longer than two seconds right now. Anyway, you and Kaylea probably want to get out of here." He kissed her on the cheek. "Miriam and I owe you for saving our son's life."

"Please, Doctor Abrams, I was only doing my job." Once more Danny pulled away from the warmth of his affection.

"Nevertheless, we're grateful." He started to leave the waiting room but stopped at the door. Without looking back at her, he said, "My son told me he hadn't seen you in some time. I hope whatever happened doesn't prevent you from coming to see us so we can thank you properly, both of us."

"Really, that's not necessary."

"Maybe not for you, but it is for us. We owe you our gratitude. And I know Miriam will want to tell you so herself." He looked around and pinned her with his gaze. "And you might want to go see Jake. Regardless of the circumstances, I'm sure he wants to thank you, too. He's been moved from the ER to a med-surg floor. He was awake a few minutes ago." Harold Abrams left before she could come up with some excuse, any reason at all, to explain why seeing Jake was a bad idea.

So, although she suspected it might be the biggest mistake of her life, as soon as Doctor Abrams senior was out of sight, Danny went to the nurses' station and asked where Jacob Abrams had been sent.

• • •

Goddamn, his head hurt. It hurt so much he was having a hard time remembering exactly what had happened. Lots of the day was foggy but he was able to get a few clear images.

The message that Kaylea called.

Going to Danny's house.

Barbara Black following him.

Why? What…wait. She'd been after Kaylea. She'd thought Jim had told Kaylea about her visits to the camps. Thought Kaylea had recognized her the day she killed the guy in Forest Park. Barbara Black was who they'd been looking for. All the time they'd been talking about "he" and it had been a "she."

Barbara had made him tie up Kaylea with something. He'd gagged her, too. Barbara was about to do something to him—maybe shoot him—when she was distracted. A phone rang, that was it. When she'd looked around for the phone, he made a move to grab her gun, then struggled with her until the gun went off and he fell.

He closed his eyes, exhausted from the effort to remember. There was more, he knew, but he needed a rest before he pushed any harder at a brain that felt like mush.

Whatever had happened next must have included a pretty hard hit to his head. He started to raise his right hand to his head only to see the IV in it with a unit of blood running wide open into him. Must have bled some.

Using his left hand he felt around his head and found a large surgical dressing. That's why his head hurt. Holy hell, the dressing covered a good part of his head. The wound must have been—must be—huge.

His thigh hurt, too. Hell, everything hurt. He should give in and slip back into sleep. But there was something hiding just out of reach at the edges of his mind that he knew he wanted to remember. But what? What?

Danny. That was it. Danny had been there. He'd been dazed by the fall, slipping in and out of semi-consciousness when he heard her voice. But he couldn't understand what she was saying. Why? Why couldn't he…oh, she wasn't speaking English. What was she saying?

He'd have to figure that out later. He had worked his brain as much as he possibly could. All he knew was he and Kaylea had been there but now he wasn't, thanks to Danny. And Sam. Sam had been there too.

God, all these bits and pieces. Nothing solid to hang on to. Only fragments. It was like being in the hospital after the IED.

Holy hell, he couldn't go there again. Not for anything. He had to hang on to something more pleasant, a better memory.

Danny. Thinking about Danny was better. He could see her leaning over him, her fingers streaked with blood. She put her hand up to his face and hushed him. Then she went on speaking It was Hebrew. That's it. She was speaking Hebrew.

She looked so worried. Maybe he was worse off than he thought. No, his father had been here and told him he was okay. Just lost some blood from the scalp wound. Dozens and dozens of stitches to close it up.

Why was Danny worried, then? If only he could believe she was worried about him.

Good God, there she was. He could see her standing at the door of his hospital room. She couldn't be real. He must be able to conjure her up by thinking about her. Her blouse and trousers were spotted with something. Blood? No matter. She was beautiful. Always so beautiful.

...

Jake did look better. Danny could see that even from the doorway. All the blood had been washed off him and the gray pallor that had convinced them all he was dead had been wiped away by a transfusion. Satisfied that he really was all right, she thought she could leave quietly. But he seemed to have seen her. He didn't say anything, though. Only stared at her. It was unnerving.

She broke the silence. "Jake? Are you okay?"

His head jerked back, as if he was startled. "Danny? Is that really you? You're here?"

"Yeah, Sam and I came over as soon as the crime scene guys got to my house. I wanted to see how you…how Kaylea was." She took a step into the room and stopped.

"She's here, too? How is she?"

"Good. She's good. They checked her over and she's fine. As soon as she signs her discharge, we'll leave."

"You won't be going home right away, I guess."

"No, I thought I'd have someone come in and get your blood off my kitchen floor before I went back to living there."

He tried to pull himself upright in bed but she could see it was a struggle. "If I need this unit of blood and all this bandaging on my head, I must have left a mess."

"What the hell happened, Jake, that you ended up bleeding all over the floor?"

"I'm a little fuzzy on the details. I think I saw a chance to get the weapon away from Barbara. We struggled. I fell. Must have hit my head."

Danny was quiet for a few moments, feeling the control she'd had over her emotions begin to slip away as her frustration about what had happened began to morph into anger. She didn't want Jake to see that she had any emotion attached to him but she had a feeling her tense shoulders and balled up fists were a dead giveaway even before she spoke.

"You know, Jake," she began, trying to control her voice, "you're a piece of work. You lecture people who know what they're doing about how they shouldn't be taking risks, then turn around and do something stupid like try to wrestle a weapon away from a killer when you're not trained to do anything like that."

He seemed taken aback by her comment. "I wouldn't say I didn't know what I was doing."

"Oh, right. I forgot. The Guard trains its docs in hand-to-hand combat."

"Of course they don't but I know how to deal with weapons."

Danny jammed her hands into her trouser pockets so she didn't give in to the impulse to wrap them around his neck. "Did it occur to you what could have happened if she'd had the presence of mind to keep pulling the trigger?"

She was sure from the look on his face that he hadn't but he wasn't going to give her the satisfaction of saying so. However, the silence that greeted her question gave her the answer.

"Do you know what would have happened to you, to Kaylea? Hell, to my kitchen? My God, Jake, you could have been..." She stopped and glared at him.

He squirmed in the bed, avoiding her eyes, picking at the sheet, looking more uncomfortable than he had when she walked in. "Well, she didn't do that," he finally said. "And as soon as I fell, I pretended to be unconscious. Then she said something that made me think she thought I was dead so I lay still and let her think that."

"Pretending you were dead was the only smart thing you did all day. You took a stupid risk by trying to disarm her. Hell, you took a stupid risk by going to my house. You should have called me. Or if you didn't want to deal with me, you should have called Sam."

By this time, Danny was pacing the floor in the room, running her hands over her face in frustration.

He seemed to want to say something but she didn't let him. It felt so good to unload all her frustration. "Didn't it seem odd to you that Barbara Black told you that Kaylea called the clinic? If she had been in trouble don't you think Kaylea would have called your cell phone? Or called me? The cop? The person she was living with?" She turned her furious gaze to him. "And how the hell did you know where she was, anyway?"

Before he could answer, she waved him off. "Never mind. I don't think I want to know. This is too fucked up for me to even…"

A nurse stuck her head in the door. "Is everything all right in here? It's getting a little loud."

Jake said, "It's okay, nurse. Detective Hartmann is asking me some questions about what happened. I'm afraid she's not happy about some of my answers."

"Well, if you could keep it down, please. You're disturbing the patients in the next room."

"We'll try," Jake said, flashing his most charming smile at her.

When the nurse had left, Jake took the opportunity to sneak in a response, "I found out where Kaylea was from Bob Aronson. He told me when I was making rounds at the camp. He thought I'd know how she was. She'd told him not to come to your place because she was afraid he'd lead the killer there."

"So, instead you did."

"Not on purpose. For God's sake, Danny, cut me some slack here. I thought I was responding to a request for my help. That's what I do."

Danny finally stopped pacing and stood next to his bed, looking him straight in the eye. "Yeah, you respond to calls for help. That's what you do. Like I do." She ran her hand over her face again. "This is old ground. I didn't mean to get into this discussion now.

I'm really only here to see for myself that you're okay, like ycur dad said. I'm glad you are. I better go and see to Kaylea." Withcut saying good-bye she walked to the door.

Jake put out his hand to her. "Danny, wait. Can't we talk?"

But she ignored him and left the room.

Chapter Eighteen

Danny took Kaylea from the hospital to the Marriot, where they stayed for three days until a company that specialized in cleaning up crime scenes got Danny's kitchen cleaner than it had been when she moved in. Kaylea didn't move back home with her, however. Social services found her a spot on the east side, away from any of the places with bad memories, and she settled into a small but pleasantly furnished apartment.

It was hard for Danny to move back into her house, with or without Kaylea. She couldn't face cooking in the kitchen. No matter how clean it was, she saw Jake's blood on the counter and floor every time she went in there. Sometimes even swore she could smell it. So for the first few nights she was back in her house, she brought take-out home with her and ate in the dining room.

Finally she decided to put on her big girl panties and cook herself a steak dinner. Wrong choice of entrée. The hunk of meat she'd spent way too much money on ended up in the garbage along with the wrapping and packaging that had altogether too much blood in it to make her comfortable.

She'd never given much thought to being a vegetarian but if this kept up she'd be one soon. A vegetarian who lived on take-out.

It didn't help that she was pissed off at herself for blowing up at Jake in his hospital room. What the hell kind of former lover… girlfriend…whatever…was she? He'd been shot and injured and she lit into him, calling him an idiot or worse. It didn't escape her notice that he'd been so out of it he didn't offer much of a defense but lay there in a very un-Jake-like manner.

Of course she hadn't heard from him since he got out. She knew he'd been discharged, because she'd checked. He'd gone home before she'd moved back to her house. Some small part of her hoped he'd call but most of her understood that, no matter what had happened in wrapping up the case, he was probably angry about how it had ended between them.

Then she talked to the Bureau's expert on PTSD about both Jake and her reaction to the recent events at her house. It made her feel worse. He explained that Jake's actions in Forest Park were to be expected from someone who had full-blown PTSD, as Jake apparently had. The counselor pointed out to Danny that her reaction to what happened in her house was a small taste of the same response. She might not have nightmares and flashbacks but she did have an emotional reaction to what had happened that played out after the event. It was not out of the ordinary.

That night, after talking to the company shrink, she sat eating her take-out Pad Thai, trying to face the fact that she was responsible for the huge hole in her life where her relationship— yes, dammit, they'd had a *relationship*—with Jake had been. She stared up from the hole she'd gotten into but didn't know if she could climb out of it and walk back from what she'd done.

The only thing that was going well was work. As Sam had predicted, Lieutenant Angel was over the moon happy with how she had handled things. L.T., as his detectives called him, was known for his calm, cool, and calculated manner with everyone from his subordinates and the press to the Chief and the Mayor. But when Danny reported for work after Barbara Black had been taken into custody, L.T. just about kissed her. He insisted she do a presser with him, took her to the Mayor's office for an official photo op with the Chief, and submitted her name for another commendation.

Danny was more interested in what they were learning from Barbara Black.

The former clinic administrator described what she'd been doing as acting as an angel of mercy to free VMSC patients with PTSD of their troubles. She'd been visiting the camps at night with boxes of food, which was how the East States Medical Supplies cardboard had gotten to the camps. The food was heavily dosed with medications like digoxin, so that the men she gave the food to, patients from the clinic, would appear to have heart attacks and die. She also added methanol to their cheap booze so if the digoxin didn't work, they would succumb to the poison. She claimed credit for a dozen deaths, none of which had been thought to be anything other than natural.

The problem arose when Jim Branson saw her one night. She was dressed in her black hooded sweatshirt and black pants but she was afraid he had recognized her. Then a few days later, at the clinic, he said something that made her sure he had. He made a joke about her food making some of the guys sick so they'd have to come into the clinic. He said that he would watch out for her from now on. She didn't think it was funny.

He had it wrong. She wasn't making anyone sick so they came into the clinic; she was trying to kill them so they wouldn't be there anymore. And he didn't seem to make the connection between the dozen deaths she'd caused and what she was doing. However, she decided to get rid of him in case he finally put two and two together. She didn't think she could get to him as she had her other victims and decided to upgrade to a gun. She bought one and used the two drive-bys as target practice before killing Jim. It turned out so well, she abandoned the poisoned food and booze and continued with the gun.

Nothing could shake her conviction that she was doing these men a favor by killing them, releasing them, she said, from their world of pain and suffering and thereby also ridding the clinic of the PTSD patients Jake had brought in against her wishes so she could regain control of her own private kingdom. She believed she should be rewarded, not punished.

They scheduled psychiatric evaluations.

•••

Once Danny had suffered through being the subject of a couple news cycles, things got back to a more normal rhythm. She threw herself into her job with a vengeance. She never got home before nine and most nights was in bed by ten, reading. She didn't take time to go out for lunch and turned down yet another invitation from Amanda and Sam to have dinner with them. If she could have, she'd have moved into Central Precinct to avoid going home to her house that was still empty of everything but bad memories.

On Friday, a week after she'd moved back into her house, she was trying to avoid thinking about the empty weekend ahead by filling the afternoon with as much work as possible. She'd made lists of the names and addresses of the witnesses in the new case she and Sam had caught and talked her partner into starting the interviews that afternoon.

She grabbed her leather case and said, "I'm ready to get this done, Sam. Are you?"

"You're sure you want to start this now? We could get some of the paperwork done on the other cases and you could go home at a decent hour for a change."

"No, I'd rather get this going. You know how I feel about going home."

"Yeah, your knack for pulling men out of kitchens where they've been shot seems to have freaked you out this time. Not so much when it was me who was bleeding all over the floor."

"Not funny, Sam." She finished loading up her leather case and zipped it up. Without looking at him she asked, "How'd you and Amanda do it? How'd you go back in her kitchen after you'd been shot there?"

He didn't respond right away and when she looked up to see why, she saw him staring into the distance, behind her, with a curious look on his face.

"Sam? You hear what I asked?" she said.

"I heard. But you have someone waiting to talk to you," he said, nodding his head in the direction of the hall.

"Who…?" Once she turned she didn't have to finish the question. Jake was standing behind her. Dressed in the jeans and cable knit sweater he always wore to the free clinic, he looked unsure of his reception and maybe a bit pale. But he still looked like the man who figured in her nightly dreams even though she had successfully blocked him out of her thoughts during the day. Mostly.

The only thing not included in her dreams was the stark white bandage over the stitches in his head and the slight limp as he walked towards her that indicated the wound in his thigh still bothered him.

"Doctor Abrams. What a surprise." She hated the squeak in her voice and fussed some more with the things on her desk until she felt like she had it under better control. "You look like you're doing okay."

"I am. Thanks to you. That's why I'm here, to thank you. I didn't get the chance to do that properly either before they hauled me off to the hospital or when you dropped in for your very brief visit. I kept hoping you'd come back so I could do the polite thing but you never did. So, here I am."

"You didn't have to come all the way here to say that. You could have called. Or not even that." She had no idea why her insides felt like they were twisted into a knot. Like her tongue was. "You could have…you know…not said anything. I was only doing my job."

"Yeah, I know. Still, I wanted to tell you myself that I appreciate how well you do it." He took his hands out of his jeans pockets and put one out to her. She ignored it. "Is there any chance I can…we can…" He took a deep breath and she realized he was as nervous as she was. "Is there someplace where we could talk privately for a few minutes?"

Danny glanced over at Sam who'd been watching them with a sympathetic expression on his face. Problem was, she didn't know if he was sympathetic to her plight or Jake's obvious discomfort. "No, not really. It's not a good time. Sam and I have a new case we need to get to work on. A ton of interviews. You probably read about it. That gang killing in southeast Portland. Lots of people around, not too many who've been very forthcoming about sharing information with us. We need to go back and try to get them to talk before…" Realizing she was running on, she stopped.

Sam interceded. "There's an empty interview room down the hall, Doc. You know where it is. It's the one we used when I talked to you. I'll wait for you, Danny. We're not in that big a hurry."

"Thanks, Sam," Jake said and gestured to her to follow him.

Well, she thought. *That answers that question. Sam's sticking with his own kind. He'll pay for this.*

She slammed her leather folder onto her desk and stalked down the hall, after Jake. Thanks to his damn long legs, he got to the room before she did, opening the door for her. He half-smiled and held his arm out, as if to say, "After you."

Storming into the room, she went almost to the opposite wall, making sure the table was between them before she faced him. "Well, Doctor Abrams, what can we do for you?"

"For starters, you can call me Jake again." He walked around the table, eliminating the only barrier between them.

"Okay, then, *Jake*, what can we do for you?"

He took a few more steps closer to her. "It's not your organization I want to talk to. It's you, personally."

"Oh, for God's sake, Jake, what the fuck do you want?"

Damn him. Getting her to lose it was apparently one of the things he was after because he grinned and looked relaxed for the first time since he got there. "I want you to listen to me grovel while I apologize for being such a fucking idiot."

Another step brought him almost directly in front of her. She backed up to keep distance between them.

"Then I want you to accept my apology even though you still might think I was an interfering asshole."

This time when he advanced toward her and she backed up, she found herself against the wall.

"After that, you can forgive me and tell me you'll give me—give us—another chance."

Now close enough that she could feel his breath on her face, he brought his mouth close to her ear. He didn't touch her, but only whispered, "Last, you can let me hold you and tell you I love you and will do anything to make it up to you for being a jerk."

Her breathing was ragged as she slid sideways, scraping against the wall, escaping what she was sure would be his next move, kissing her.

"Jake, this isn't the time or the place for this. We're not alone."

He looked around the empty room, a puzzled frown on his face. "There's no one here but us, Danny."

"Not in the room there isn't. But that's one-way glass over there and I'm willing to bet half the precinct is behind it watching us." She looked over at the window and raised her voice slightly. "And, although I have my doubts, there might be one among them with the intelligence to figure out how to flip the switch that lets them hear us, too, although they'd probably have to call IT for help figuring it out."

Another grin split his face. "Sam sent us into this room on purpose, didn't he?"

"Yes, I imagine a scene like this is what he was hoping for." She smiled for the first time since he'd cornered her.

"That's better, you're smiling," he said softly as he backed up a step, giving her room to breathe. "Okay, if you don't want to put on a show for your colleagues, what time are you off tonight? Let me come pick you up and buy you a drink or, better yet, dinner. That'll give me lots of time to grovel."

"I'm not sure when I'll be finished those interviews. It might be late. And dinner's probably not a good idea. Besides, it's Friday. Aren't you expected at your parents' house?"

"Nothing takes precedence over apologizing to you. Please, let me at least buy you a drink." He was pleading now.

"How about I call you when I get home? We can talk then."

"Not what I hoped for but…You promise you'll call?"

"I promise."

He leaned down and pressed his lips against her forehead in a gentle kiss, which almost undid her resolve not to touch him. She wanted to throw herself into his arms, hold him close, kiss him like she really meant it. She'd missed him so much.

However, she still wasn't convinced he could accept who she was at work, who she needed to be so she didn't lose herself in the relationship he wanted. And that was a deal breaker. Until she knew, she had to stay away from him.

He touched her face with the back of his hand. "I'll talk to you tonight, baby." And he left the room.

She waited a few seconds before saying, "If I see anyone in the hall when I come out of this room, and that especially means you, Richardson, your ass is grass and I'm a lawn mower. Got it?"

The hall was empty when she walked out. But from the studied way everyone avoided looking at her when she went back to her desk, she'd been wrong. Half the precinct hadn't been watching. The whole damn lot of them had been.

Chapter Nineteen

Danny stood across the street from her target for at least ten minutes, trying to decide if she should hit it or not. What finally decided her was the sudden onslaught of cold rain sweeping across the street, soaking through her clothes in seconds. She pulled the hood on her raincoat up over her head, which did nothing other than add a bit more water to what was already dripping down her neck.

She either had to get back to the streetcar and head for home or cross the street and take shelter there. And if the chicken was brave enough to cross the road, how could she not? Dodging the traffic that was always heavy on Northwest 23rd on a Friday night, she got to the other side, ran up to the target's door, and knocked.

There was no answer.

After a second knock that wasn't any more successful at getting a response than the first one was, she was about to leave when she heard someone talking inside, moving toward the door. From pauses between the sentences, she thought she was hearing one side of a phone conversation. As the person came closer to the door it was obvious that she was correct.

"I can't. No, probably not at all. Look, I gotta go. Someone's knocking at the…" The door opened. Jake stopped talking. He stared at her for what seemed like the longest time. Then he said, "I'll call you later, Mom," punched a button, and jammed the phone in his jeans pocket.

"Thank God. I'd about given up on you. I was sure I'd blown it going to the precinct. Embarrassing you. I thought I'd never see you again." He closed his eyes and sighed. "I'm such an idiot. I don't know why I should expect you to ever forgive me. Everything I do gives me one more thing to apologize for."

Surely he could see she was shivering. And couldn't he hear her teeth chattering? Why was he standing there staring at her? When he didn't say anything more, she asked, "Can I come in? It's really wet out here."

He seemed to see for the first time how drenched she was. "Holy hell, I can't even do this right. I'm sorry. Of course you can come in." She took a step into the entry hall—and was swept into his arms where he held her, rocking her gently, murmuring endearments. She heard him say "sorry" at least three times and "forgive me" four.

"Jake, I'm dripping all over you and your wood floors," she protested, pulling away from him.

"Fuck the wood floors. You came here because I said I needed to grovel. So let me." He held her by the shoulders and started talking. "I'm sorry, Danny. I was wrong, dead wrong. You were right. I overreacted. The only excuse I have is that seeing him… her…with a weapon pointed at you triggered something I thought I'd put in the past." He kissed her forehead. "I've been working with my shrink again. For the first few sessions I kept insisting I was right to tackle you. But he's convinced me it was my PTSD back again. Can you ever forgive me?"

When she said nothing, he looked beseechingly in her eyes. "Please don't tell me you're here to say it's all over. Tell me you've forgiven me. That you'll give me—give us—another chance."

She smiled. "Yeah, I'm here for a little of that. A little of 'I'm sorry, too.' I talked to the Bureau's expert on PTSD. He agreed that you probably had a flashback or something like that and it brought an automatic response, like the one you'd have had in Iraq. I should have known what it was. I should have been more understanding. It's not as if I haven't seen PTSD before."

"You have nothing to be sorry for but if you want, my people can talk to your people and tell us what we should do. What do you think?" His blue eyes lit up with humor as he hugged her again.

"I don't think we need the middle men. I think we can just talk to each other, figure this out between us." She shivered. Even with his body heat she was chilled to the bone from the cold rain.

"I like your plan. But before we talk, you need some dry clothes. You can borrow some of mine. They'll be too big but it'll be better than…"

She looked up at him. "I think what you meant to say was, 'let me get you out of those wet clothes,' didn't you?"

"Is that what I meant?" He grinned. "See, when you're not around for a while, I can't even remember how to get you naked. How about a soak in the spa tub? That should warm you up."

"Yes, please. That's what I need. And a martini. Any chance for that?"

"Coming up. But first things first. Let's get your wet coat and gloves off."

She kicked off her soaked shoes and yanked at the leather gloves she was wearing, now so wet they clung to her hands as if the leather was her skin. "Damn, I can't get them off."

"Here, let me." He took her left hand and rolled the bottom of the glove up over her palm. Gently he tugged the glove off her thumb and kissed the pad at the base. Next he moved to her index finger and did the same thing.

One finger at a time, he peeled the wet leather gloves off her hands, kissing the base of each finger when it was freed, never once saying a word. By the time he was finished with his slow strip of both hands, although she was still fully clothed, she felt more naked and exposed than she had ever felt. And she could see from the dark storm in his eyes that he felt the same.

Still without saying anything he went behind her and slipped her raincoat from her shoulders, sliding it down her back slowly, brushing the base of her neck with feathery kisses. Then he led her to the Jacuzzi and, while the water was running to fill the tub, began to carefully remove her turtleneck sweater and wool pants until she was standing in front of him clad only in her pale yellow lace bra and panties.

Finally he spoke. "Would you take it to mean I only love you for your body if I told you I missed seeing you like this?" he asked.

She laughed. "No, not if you forgive me for saying I really missed this." And she pressed herself against him, her arms around his neck, and took ownership of his mouth with a deep, passionate kiss that made her toes curl and sucked the breath from her lungs. The kiss was so hot she almost forgot she was chilled to the bone.

By the time they had each regained the ability to stand without holding on to the other, the tub was full. She shed her underwear and, taking his hand, stepped in and sank back into the warm water. It wasn't until she heard his sharp intake of breath that she realized her breasts were above the water line, her nipples still contracted into hard points from the cold and their kiss.

"Are you going to stand there looking or are you going to join me?"

"I'll never get enough of looking at you. You are beautiful. But there was a request for a martini. Why don't you relax for ten minutes while I go get that taken care of?"

Before she could object he was gone. She turned on the jets and slid further down into the warm water and let them work their magic. It was glorious. The tension of the past weeks floated away as the water pulsed against her muscles.

She was almost on the edge of a cat nap when she heard Jake say, "If I join you, can I get the groveling out of the way real fast before I get too distracted by the sea goddess who's sharing the hot tub with me?" He was taking off his shirt as he spoke. He'd pulled a small stool next to the tub and on it were two cocktail glasses containing their martinis.

Holding out her hand, she said, "Come grovel away."

In what seemed like only seconds, he finished undressing and was sitting beside her, his arm around her, her leg over his, her head on his shoulder.

He picked up a glass, handed it to her, then picked up the second one and raised it in a toast. "L'chaim."

"To life, indeed." She touched her glass to his and then took a sip. "Okay, finish the groveling so we can get to the good part."

He took a big sip of his drink. "I finally get it, Danny. What you did with Kaylea and Barbara Black, handling that without ever putting anyone at risk, was a revelation. I'm sorry it took a crisis to make me understand. But I do. I am now officially in love with every bit of you. The woman, the cop, the person who can rebuild a VW engine, who can impress my parents in less than an hour. The whole beautiful package. What you do is a huge part of you and I'd never change that." He kissed the top of her head. "If you forgive me, I promise I'll never do anything like that again. I was a jackass and I'm sorry."

She turned his face so they were looking, staring really, into each other's eyes. What she saw was what she needed to see—his sincerity, his regret, and, most of all, his love. "I'm sorry, too. I should have known what was going on. The Bureau's shrink got me to see that. If I hadn't been so afraid I'd lose who I am in a relationship with you, maybe I'd have seen it sooner. And you're not a jackass. I'd never be in love with a jackass. So you can't be one. Because I love you, Jake."

She heard his breath stutter. "As long as I've wanted to hear that, now that you've said it, I'm not so sure I deserve it, deserve you."

"Hey, you're stealing my lines again," she said.

"I'm serious, Danny. I still feel like I…"

"When I told you I didn't deserve you, you said I should be with a super hero or some star athlete. Well, back at you. You'd be better off with some movie star or Nobel laureate who's beautiful, brilliant, and accomplished. But you're not gonna find out what that's like. Because I have you and I'm not letting you go. I think that was the gist of your response and I'm stealing it."

He threw his head back and laughed, a deep, belly laugh. "Damn, baby, do you remember every conversation that well?"

"Yup. Keep that in mind for the future. I'll always remember what you say."

He took the now empty glass from her hand and put it, along with his, back on the stool. "Now, groveling over. Let's get to the…what did you call it? The good part?"

"Actually, the groveling isn't over."

"You mean I need to do more?"

"No, I need to do some. I'm embarrassed by how I talked to you in the hospital. You'd been injured, hauled out of my kitchen on a gurney, had your head stitched back together, and I yelled at you so loud the nurse had to intervene. I wasn't sure I could face you again after I left. I'm sorry. Can you forgive me for that?"

"Didn't bother me a bit."

"Really? I was a bitch. Weren't you pissed at me?"

"No, I wasn't. You were angry, that was obvious. But it was a relief. I figured you wouldn't have been that angry if you didn't care about me. It gave me hope we could work this out between us."

"Then why the hell didn't you call sometime in the past week? I kept hoping you would."

"And you couldn't do the same?"

"I did. I called the hospital but you were already discharged. And I called the clinic to see if you were back to work yet."

"Hmm. But not me."

"No, not you. I told you, I was too embarrassed by my ranting."

She heard the sound of his ringtone coming from the jeans he'd dropped on the floor. "Bet that's your mom wondering why you didn't call her back."

"Oh, hell, I forgot. She was calling about dinner."

He finally got the phone from where he'd stashed it and looked at the screen. "Good call, baby." He answered. "Hi, Mom? Sorry. I was waiting for…Yeah, that's who I was waiting for. Uh-huh, she's here. Okay." He handed the phone to her. "My mom wants to talk to you." He raised an eyebrow and smirked. Mouthing, "Good luck," he settled back in the tub and tweaked her nipple trying, she knew, to distract her.

"Hi, Miriam," Danny began, swatting away his hand.

"Danny, I've been thinking of you so much over the past ten days. I should have called to thank you."

"You don't need to…"

"Of course I do. You saved my son. I'll be forever in your debt. A mother's debt. If you ever have children, not that you have to but if you ever do, you'll understand."

"I was doing my job."

"And thank God you do it so well." She paused for a breath finally. "Has my son fed you dinner yet?"

"No, we…ah…we've been talking."

"Oh, is that what you call it now? It used to be called making love. Or having sex. Or that other word I never use." Danny had to move the phone away so Miriam couldn't hear her laugh. When she got herself under control, she went back to the conversation. Jake's mom was saying, "…drive you here. I made enough food tonight for my whole family and it turned out my granddaughter has an ear infection, so David and his family didn't come and Jacob was apparently waiting for you. So he could apologize, I hope, for being fool enough to let you go."

"Miriam, I…"

"Let me talk to him, please."

She handed the phone back to Jake who said, "Uh-huh" a couple times then said, "I love you, too," before hanging up. "She expects us there for dinner in an hour. Do you mind? She says she wants to thank you in person."

"Dinner's fine," Danny said. She settled back against his shoulder. "She thinks she interrupted us having sex, you know."

Jake drew her onto his lap so she straddled him and began to caress her breasts. "In that case, we better do something about it. I've always tried to live up to my parents' expectations. Although it took me a long time to find the nice Jewish girl they always wanted me to find." He reached over the side of the tub and felt around. "I think there's another condom here from the last time we were in the tub." He brought up a foil packet.

"How convenient," she said as she tore it open.

"It's been waiting for you."

"Wait's over, lover."

From the Author

I hope you enjoyed *Believing Again*, book number five in the Second Chances series. If you liked meeting Jake and Danny, you might enjoy *Beginning Again* (Liz and Collins), *Loving Again*, (Sam and Amanda), *Together Again* (Tony and Margo), or *Trusting Again* (Cynthia and Marius). Oh, and book six in the series (Nick and Fiona) will be released early in 2014.

If you'd like to keep in touch, here are a few places where you can find me:

My website and blog: *www.peggybirdwrites.com*

On Facebook: *https://www.facebook.com/peggybirdauthor*

On Twitter: *https://twitter.com/peggybirdwrites*

On Pinterest: *http://pinterest.com/writingbird/*

One last thing: I always like to know what readers think of my books. So if you'd write a review on Amazon or Goodreads with your honest opinion, I'd appreciate it. Thanks so much.

More from This Author
(From *Trusting Again* by Peggy Bird)

"I love it when she has the men in the audience sing the chorus to 'Eight Miles Wide,'" Liz Fairchild said. "Hearing deep voices sing about the size of their vaginas never fails to amuse me."

Cynthia Blaine had known Liz for years and, although she wasn't surprised by anything the other woman said, she was sometimes still astonished by where Liz chose to say it. However, shushing her was a waste of effort. So was pointing out the startled expressions of the people who'd heard the comment. Liz had never learned to care about keeping her voice down or her opinion to herself.

"You like saying that out loud, don't you?" Cynthia said.

"No one objects to that word anymore, do they? And if they do, maybe it'll clear out the place so we can get a table. Otherwise, we're out of luck. The bar's full," Liz said.

They'd just come from a matinee of the Oregon Symphony featuring Storm Large, a performer with a great voice and an amazing repertoire of songs, not all of which were appropriate for the faint of heart, a category which included Liz's favorite, her signature song. Now, standing at the entrance to the Heathman Hotel bar, the women were hoping to find a table so they could have a glass of wine.

This girls' afternoon out also included Amanda St. Claire, who was doing a recon for a table in the back. Amanda hadn't been out much since the birth of her baby and Liz, whose art gallery exhibited both Amanda's art glass and Cynthia's designer jewelry, had, as she described it, "arranged the excursion to rectify that."

Amanda rejoined them just in time to catch the last part of the conversation. "It's full there, too," she said waving toward the other room. "There are three empty chairs at a table for four, but there was a guy sitting there. I guess he's waiting for people to join him."

"Did you ask?" Liz said.

"No, it seemed rude."

"If he has the only empty chairs in the place, it's not rude. If you can't do it, I will." Liz headed to the area that served as overflow bar, tearoom, and place to lunch for the hotel restaurant.

In a few minutes, she reappeared in the door to the back room and motioned to the other two to join her.

"Oh, my God. Did we get lucky," she said in a low voice. "And not just by scoring a table. The man we'll be sitting with is one of the most beautiful creatures ever to walk the planet."

"So, Liz, when did you say Collins will be back in Portland?" Amanda asked, trailing behind Cynthia.

"I didn't and you're usually more subtle than that. I love Collins but I'm not blind. You'll understand when you see this man," Liz said. "And to answer your question, however rhetorical it may have been, this is his week in Portland. He should be home now. With any luck, he'll even have dinner—"

"Holy hell." Cynthia stopped so suddenly, Amanda ran into the back of her. "Is that the guy you're talking about?" She nodded toward a man sitting alone at a table for four, a glass of red wine in his hand.

"Yup, isn't he gorgeous?" Liz asked.

"I know him," Cynthia said. "He commissioned a piece of my jewelry a month or so ago for his girlfriend."

"Damn. There goes my plan to set you up. I figured I might find a way for Amanda and me to leave without you so he'd ask you to dinner."

"Don't you dare do anything like that," Cynthia said, raising her voice slightly and emphasizing the "dare" part of the sentence. The last thing she needed was Liz's heavy-handed matchmaking. It was uncomfortable enough when Liz tried to fix her up with one of her artists. Cynthia definitely didn't want any attempts to get her together with this man.

Not when he woke up a hatch of butterflies in her stomach every time she thought about him. Ever since he'd walked into the Erickson Gallery, she'd been full of fluttery things on a regular basis. As she was now.

She smoothed the skirt of her plain lavender linen maxi dress, trying to get rid of the wrinkles, then tied the ends of the deep purple shrug she wore over it a little tighter around her waist. It was too late to wish she'd worn something sexier. Or had put her tawny blonde hair up in some intricate roll, rather than a simple braid down the middle of her back. Worn fuck-me shoes instead of the flat sandals she had on. Put on a little more make-up; put on any make-up at all.

Oh, for God's sake. Wearing something else wouldn't have made any difference. He has a girlfriend. One he spent big bucks on for a birthday present. And what the hell was she thinking, anyway? Even if he wasn't attached, he was way out of her league. After the whole Josh disaster last year, she'd vowed never to get herself in a similar situation again. She'd barely gotten out of that relationship with any shred of ego intact.

As the three women approached the table, the subject of her fantasies stood to greet them. Cynthia was sure his picture was in the dictionary next to the phrase "tall, dark, and handsome." Cliché it may be but, in his case, true. He was well over six feet tall, with skin the color of a latte, and thick, black-brown hair that curled around his ears and at the back of his neck. The first time she'd seen him in Seattle, she'd immediately wanted to thread her fingers through that hair. Lick up the side of his neck until she got to his jaw line, an earlobe, his full-lipped mouth, whatever she could reach to kiss. Put her arms over those broad shoulders. Earn one of those sensuous smiles.

Everything about the man was burned into her brain including what was, she was pretty sure from watching it walk away from her, the best ass in the Northwest. So she knew if she wasn't careful, before this little unexpected encounter in Portland had ended, she'd likely be drooling all over him like a St. Bernard.

When the man recognized Cynthia, a broad grin spread over his face and lit up his brown eyes. "If I'd known you were one of the women who were table-less, I'd have carried it out to you. With a bottle of champagne."

"So, the birthday gift was a success," Cynthia said.

"Absolutely," he said. "It was the hit of the evening. I've been out of town on business or I would have let you know how much my friend appreciated it." He turned the smile on the other two women. "Sorry. Didn't mean to be rude. I'm Marius Hernandez. Cynthia created an amazing piece of jewelry for me to give a friend as a birthday present."

"This is Liz Fairchild, Marius. She has a gallery in Portland where I have some of my work. And this is Amanda St. Claire. She shows her work at The Fairchild, too."

"Everyone knows Amanda St. Claire's art glass. And I've read about your gallery, Liz. I don't know what I've done to deserve the pleasure of three beautiful and talented women joining me but whatever it was, I hope I do it often." He gestured toward the table. "Please. Sit. Let me flag down a server and get you something to drink."

Liz took the chair next to Marius and Amanda sat opposite her, leaving the place across from him for Cynthia. She moved the chair back from the table a bit, sure that if he went back to the slouch he'd been in before he stood, she'd be brushing knees with him and she didn't think she could handle that.

But instead of inhabiting the chair with a casual sprawl, he sat up straighter, his forearms on the table in front of him which put her hands, not her knees, in danger. Even without touching him,

Cynthia was unnerved by being this close to him. She played with the strap of the shoulder bag in her lap, twisting her fingers in it, trying not to watch him. But she wasn't able to keep herself from sneaking peeks at him out of the corner of her eye.

"Cyn, what do you want?" Amanda's voice broke through the heated mist that had obscured every other thought as soon as she'd seen Marius. "We've ordered our drinks and some food to share. The server's waiting for you."

"Sorry, a glass of house red, please."

"Make that a bottle of the Malbec I'm drinking," Marius said to the server before asking Cynthia, "Is that okay with you? I'm drinking red wine, too, and with you and Liz ordering red, it makes sense to have a bottle."

"I've never had a Malbec," she said, "but sure. Sounds fine."

"Most Northwesterners who drink red wine stick to local pinot noirs. But this is one of my favorites. It's from Argentina, from a high altitude vineyard in the Andes. I think you'll like it."

"So, Marius, now that we have that settled," Liz began, clearly finished with the wine discussion, "I'd love to know more about you. You commissioned a piece from Cynthia in Seattle, but are hanging out in Portland. Do you live in Washington or Oregon? Or do you slide back and forth across the Columbia at will?"

He seemed to take Liz in stride, merely smiling at her as he answered. "I live in Seattle. I'm in Portland for a coffee convention."

"There are conventions for coffee?" Liz said. "Who knew?"

"Coffee's big business. Especially now that Starbucks has taken it out of the supermarket and made it gourmet. My family has been in the business for several generations and we've seen the change. Benefited from it, to be honest."

"You sell coffee?" Liz asked.

"Not in the sense I think you mean. We're brokers for coffee plantation owners in Central America. We arrange the deals between coffee roasters here and plantations there."

"Coffee roasters like Starbucks?"

"Don't I wish. No, we have several dozen clients in and around Portland, same in Seattle, and a growing number in California."

"Is your family in Seattle?" Amanda asked.

"Miami. My family came from Cuba when Castro took over." Before Liz could ask another question, he went on, "My grandfather started the business. My father and uncles run it now and my brother, a cousin, and I are next in line. I was sent to Seattle to open a West Coast office to handle all the business your coffee culture was bringing us. It's only me, a couple computers, and an assistant but…" His self-deprecating smile didn't really match the rest of his confident body language.

Which was what Cynthia was staring at—his body. Especially his shoulders. His gorgeous shoulders were clad in a jacket that never wrinkled when he moved, like it was part of his skin. She was sure he had his suits made for him. The one he wore today was brown, the perfect complement to his milky-coffee skin. The fabric looked expensive, imported from someplace like Italy. His cream-colored shirt had French cuffs held together with chunky gold cuff links. She wanted to touch the fabric of the shirt; it looked so soft, so smooth. Maybe it was silk, like his tie, which she thought was Prada.

What the hell was wrong with her? First obsessing about her clothes, now his? What men wore had never been of any interest to her. Women's clothes barely held her attention for more than the ten minutes it took for her to throw on jeans and a T-shirt every morning. She had to pull herself together. Liz and Amanda were having a normal conversation with this man while she sat like a lump, too busy thinking about things like his clothes—or what was under them—to say anything, much less anything intelligent.

"I guess you must find Seattle a bit of a change from Miami," Amanda was saying when Cynthia tuned back into the conversation.

"You have no idea. Just about everything's different, from the weather to people's idea of fun to the politics. I've gotten to like it now. Except for the beaches. Even after two years, I still miss Florida beaches."

The wine arrived; he tasted and approved it. The conversation went on, mostly around Cynthia not with her. She'd made some progress toward normalcy—she'd stopped obsessing about his clothes. Now, she was intent on making sure no part of her body touched any part of his. When he handed her a glass of wine, she took it without coming in contact with his hand. She kept her knees clenched tightly together and primly set to the side of her chair so there was no chance they would brush his. She avoided eye contact.

But the one thing she couldn't get away from was the smell of his aftershave or cologne or, who knows, maybe pheromones, wafting across the table. He smelled like some exotic spice she couldn't name. She had never, in her entire life, smelled anything that good. It was irresistible. Like every other part of him was, from the crown of his head to the just-got-out-of-bed dark stubble on his cheeks and jaw that would feel wonderfully scratchy on her skin. From the body under that custom-made suit she'd stopped thinking about until now, when she started thinking about it again, to his voice that was like a good piece of music, deep and resonant, layered with meaning. And his eyes, oh God, his eyes ...

"Cyn, is something wrong? You're so quiet." Amanda sounded concerned.

Before she could answer, Cynthia caught the expression on Marius's face. Damn. He knew exactly why she was quiet, why she was sitting like some well-behaved schoolgirl. It seemed those brown eyes could see into her heart and soul.

"I was thinking about a new piece I'm working on. Sorry."

He raised an eyebrow and buried his half-smile in his glass of wine.

"Is this for my gallery or are you going to waste it on that place in Seattle where you still have your work?" Liz asked.

"It's a commission that came from Max's gallery, that place where the owner has been as good to me in Seattle as you've been to me in Portland. And didn't I just bring you my Victorian neckpieces no one else has seen?"

"I guess I'll take that as some sort of atonement for giving him your Cleopatra collars first. Not that anyone in Seattle would ever appreciate anything like that."

A Cleopatra collar was exactly what Marius had commissioned from her, but demonstrating he was as smart as he was sexy, he only winked at her and stayed out of the discussion.

The conversation moved on to subjects less likely to make her discomfited. In response to his questions, Amanda explained to Marius some of the fine points of kiln-formed glass art. In return, he answered hers about coffee buying. In her usual outrageously flirty manner, Liz encouraged him to come to her gallery before he returned to Seattle. Cynthia said little unless prompted by her friends and even then made only brief comments, still tongue-tied by sitting across from him.

An hour later, Marius glanced at an expensive-looking watch, re-buttoned the top button of his shirt, tightened his tie and apologized for having to leave for a business dinner. Before he left, he shook the hand of each of the three women, seeming to linger with Cynthia longer than with the other two. At least it felt like he lingered, taking her smaller hand between both of his, holding it in what felt more like the clasp of a lover's hand than a good-bye handshake. She noticed, as she had when they first met, that in spite of the beautiful clothes, he had calluses on his hands that could only come from some kind of physical work. It added an aspect to him that fascinated her even more.

She hoped he hadn't noticed how her hand trembled when he held it.

• • •

Marius couldn't believe his luck. He'd been trying to find a way to get back to the Erickson Gallery for weeks so he could do what he should have done when he'd picked up the gift for a family friend—ask the beautiful artist who'd made the piece to have dinner with him. But he'd been traveling on business for most of the past month, ending up in Portland, where he'd been bored and counting the days until he could get back to Seattle.

Until he decided to kill time before his dinner meeting with a glass of wine. And there she was.

In only two brief encounters, Cynthia Blaine had managed to intrigue him. Curvy where most of the women he'd met lately had been long and lean, her face was clean of make-up, her eyes clear of calculation about what his net worth might be. He had his pick of arm candy, but going to dinner with women who were conventionally beautiful, fashionably dressed, and often more ambitious than he was—which was saying quite a lot—had worn thin. Not that he was looking for a long-term commitment. But someone real seemed like a nice change. And Cynthia Blaine was that—real and talented and beautiful.

When he'd first met her, he'd thought she was equally attracted. But he had wondered if she'd written him off because he was obviously buying a piece of expensive jewelry for a woman even though he kept emphasizing it was for a *friend*, hoping she'd get the inference. Today he thought the message must have gotten through. The way she'd flushed when he smiled at her, held her body back from touching him, looked away so he wouldn't know she'd been staring at him all seemed to say she felt the same attraction.

What he hadn't been able to do was cut her out of her herd of friends without being too obvious or obnoxious. So, he scribbled a note on the back of a business card and left it with the server when he had the bill for the women's drinks charged to his room. She assured him she'd get it to the woman in the purple dress with the long braid.

• • •

Marius was barely out the door before Liz turned on her friend.

"Cynthia, what the hell is wrong with you? Why didn't you tell us about him?"

"Why would I tell you about him? He was just another customer," she replied. "Can I have the last bit of that cheese?" She reached for the plate. Liz pushed it out of her reach.

"Don't change the subject. How could you not think we'd be interested in one of the most handsome men ever put on this earth?"

"Don't be ridiculous." She tried for the cheese plate again. And failed, thanks to Liz's determination. "I just sold him a neckpiece for his girlfriend."

"The girlfriend part, I grant you, is a shame. But, my God, girl, just run down the list of the other virtues: killer good-looking, charming, polite, interested in what we have to say, willing to ignore phone calls while he talked to us, the good taste and money to commission work from you and buy that suit. What's not worth talking about on that list?"

"I guess I wasn't paying attention."

Liz snorted. "Right. You were stunned into silence just sitting across from him."

"No, I wasn't."

"Don't bother, petal. No one will believe you. It was too obvious. Not that I blame you. You could drown in those eyes. And his smile gave me some idea of what it'll feel like when I get old enough to have hot flashes." She fanned herself to make her point more obvious.

176

"Did you notice his hands?" Amanda asked. "I love the way he talks with them. They're so big and graceful. I bet he could palm a basketball with them."

Cynthia's hand was still trembling from the handshake. Oh, yeah, she'd noticed his hands all right.

"A basketball? Honey, he could palm anything I have with them," Liz said. As the other two women burst into giggles, she added, "Please don't repeat that in front of Collins. He doesn't have much of a sense of humor when I make comments like that."

A half hour later, Liz went to pay the bill and learned that Marius had taken care of it, adding one more item to her list of reasons Marius Hernandez was God's gift to the world. The three women parted at the parking garage across the street from the concert venue, Liz headed for Southwest Portland where the man she lived with waited; Amanda to Northeast Portland, her husband and her new baby, and Cynthia for the freeway back to Seattle.

• • •

The dinner hostess at the Heathman always rearranged the desk to suit the way she liked things before she started her shift. Tonight, while she was moving things around, she found a business card with a note written on the back. No one seemed to know who it was for or why it was there. She pitched it into the recycling.

In the mood for more Crimson Romance?

Check out *Collared for a Night*
by Susan Arden
at *CrimsonRomance.com*.